DATE DUE

MR 4'99	JA 10	JA 30'06
MR 17'99	MY 31'99	DE 11'08
MR 27'99	JY	FE 05'10
JE 2 9'00	JY 6'01	JE
JY 2 4'00	JY 27'01	OC 24'13
	AG 13'01	
AP 25'00	DE 7'00	
AG 10'00	AP 9'02	
SE 6'00	OC 23'02	
OC 25'00	AG 22 03	
DE 27'00	JY 22 04	
	NO 21'08	

F
TR   Brinkerhoff, Shirley
        Balancing act
        The Nikki Sheridan
        Series #4

DEMCO

Balancing Act
Copyright © 1998
Shirley Brinkerhoff

Cover illustration by Cheri Bladholm

A Focus on the Family book.
Published by Bethany House Publishers
A Ministry of Bethany Fellowship International
11400 Hampshire Avenue South
Minneapolis, Minnesota 55438
www.bethanyhouse.com

Printed in the United States of America by
Bethany Press International, Minneapolis, Minnesota 55438

Library of Congress Cataloging-in-Publication Data

Brinkerhoff, Shirley
    Balancing act / Shirley Brinkerhoff.
        p.   cm. — (Nikki Sheridan series ; bk. 4)
    Summary: Because she suspects that Carly has an eating disorder, Nikki tries to help her friend while she also learns to address her own lack of self-acceptance by turning to God in prayer.
    ISBN 1–56179–559–3
    [1. Self-acceptance—Fiction. 2. Eating disorders—Fiction.
3. Friendship—Fiction. 4. Christian life—Fiction.] I. Title.
II. Series: Brinkerhoff, Shirley. Nikki Sheridan series ; 4.
PZ7.B780115Bal   1998
[Fic]—dc21   98–35174
                                                              CIP
                                                              AC

98 99 00 01 02 03 04 05 / 15 14 13 12 11 10 9 8 7 6 5 4 3 2 1

To John and Debbie Gordon,
with love and appreciation for
all their support and encouragement.

❦ One ❦

NIKKI SHERIDAN THOUGHT LATER that she would never have even noticed the bouquet stuck into the chain-link fence if Carly hadn't acted so totally out of character.

The air-conditioning in Aunt Marta's white Taurus had gone on the blink 30 miles back, somewhere on the winding, corkscrew roads of the Appalachian mountains. Now the three of them were dripping sweat in the stifling car, even with all four windows down, as they sat impatiently at the stop sign in Wald's Ford, Virginia. Aunt Marta's long fingers tapped an impatient rhythm on the black vinyl of the steering wheel, waiting as a rusty red pickup meandered slowly down the block toward the intersection. Nikki fanned herself with the map of Wyoming that had worked itself loose from the atlas and prayed for the air to stir just a little.

At the last minute, instead of going straight through the intersection, the truck took a sharp right onto the road beside them. Nikki barely had time to scan the "$1000 OBO" scrawled in white paint across its side window before Carly shocked her by shouting out the Taurus's open window.

"Hey! What's the matter with you? You never heard of

1

turn signals?" She pulled her head back inside the car, crossed her arms over her chest with a flounce, and muttered, "Dumb redneck!"

Three things happened in quick succession. The truck lurched to a halt, shifted with a *clank* into reverse, and backed up until it was even with the Taurus.

Marta hissed, "Carly, are you *crazy?"*

Nikki cowered in her seat, cringing at what she knew was about to happen.

The truck's rust-rimmed door flew open with a loud, metallic squawk. Feet clad in dusty black cowboy boots came into view first, followed by grease-spotted jeans and a sleeveless T-shirt that had once been white. A small man jumped to the pavement and strutted over to the Taurus.

"You there! You got some problem 'bout the way I drive?"

Dark bristles outlined the man's bony chin and shaded the hollows of his cheeks. He gripped the edge of Carly's window, which she was frantically struggling to roll up, and Nikki noted the grease that darkened his jagged fingernails and lined the creases of his knuckles.

"Well?" the man demanded. "I b'lieve one of you had something to say to me. Jus' speak right up now—I'm here."

Marta opened her door reluctantly and slid out from behind the steering wheel. Her voice was controlled, but Nikki could detect the tremor beneath her words.

"I'm very sorry," she began. "Carly shouldn't have yelled at you that way and—"

"I'll say she shouldn't've yelled at me!" the man roared back, cutting her off.

He stood no more than five-and-a-half-feet tall, Nikki estimated, and when he found he had to look up to Marta, his tone became even more hostile.

"That what you teach these kids of yours?" he growled. "How to sass?"

"They're not my kids!"

Carly sat stiff and still in the backseat, her brown eyes wide beneath the blonde bangs that nearly brushed her eyebrows. Nikki did what she'd learned to do years ago, during her parents' endless arguments back home in Ohio—she disconnected from the words flying back and forth and fixed her attention on something else, something neutral. In this case, it was the bouquet of orange and yellow marigolds and purple nasturtiums wrapped in a white paper lace doily and tied with an orange ribbon.

Weird, Nikki mused, forcing herself to focus on the flowers. *Why would anybody go to all the trouble to make a bouquet, then stick it in a rusty chain-link fence in front of a deserted gas station?*

But even her thoughts couldn't completely shut out the angry words flying in the background.

"You better learn to keep them gals under control, ma'am. That's all I got to say!"

Except it wasn't. He strode around to the front of the Taurus and peered at the license plate. "Huh! Just like I thought—not from around here."

Nikki thought he looked for all the world like a mean little rooster, with his grimy hands on his waist, elbows jutting out to either side, and head bobbing back and forth as he lectured.

Marta folded her arms. "What on earth does that have to do with anything—?"

But the Rooster broke in again. "People 'round here got better sense'n to let their kids go hollering out car windows at strangers."

"I told you before, they're not my kids."

"Then what're you doin', driving somebody else's kids

around and teaching 'em to yell at people?"

"That's ridiculous! I didn't *teach* her to yell. Carly's 16 years old—she's the daughter of friends of mine. And . . . and she's very good friends with Nikki, my niece and—" Marta gestured to where Nikki sat in the front seat, but the angry man cut in.

"Lady, I don't want to hear your family history, and I don't care whose kids you're drivin' around. I'm just telling you, you got a responsibility here, understand? Lemme tell you what *I'd* do if some kid of mine sassed that way—"

Nikki held her breath as she listened to Marta sigh slowly through clenched teeth.

Don't lose it now, Aunt Marta, Nikki thought. But her aunt surprised her. She smiled at the little man and spoke graciously as Nikki listened in amazement.

"Thanks very much for offering. But you're right—this is my responsibility, and I'll take care of it."

The Rooster finally climbed back into the cab, and his truck roared to life. It wasn't until he had driven out of sight that Nikki straightened up in her seat. At the same time, Marta walked back to the car and turned toward Carly. She leaned into the Taurus, her knee on the front seat, and glared at the girl in the back.

"Carly! What*ever* possessed you to yell at someone that way?"

Carly hesitated. Nikki thought from the look on her face that she might burst into tears. Instead, she fought for control, then lifted her chin and stared back at Marta, her voice defensive.

"I was just kidding around. He overreacted, that's all."

Marta's eyes opened wide. "I can't believe you, Carly Allen! People are getting *shot* for less than that these days."

Carly rolled her eyes. "Oh, come on, Marta. How was I supposed to know he'd be such a hotheaded redneck—?"

Marta's lips had closed in a tight line as she listened, but now she broke into Carly's words. "That's enough. I don't know where you learned to pigeonhole people that way, Carly, but I really don't appreciate it. Just let me say that as long as you're traveling with me, you don't *ever* do anything so harebrained again. Understand?"

Carly and Marta stared at one another until finally, reluctantly, Carly dropped her eyes and gave in with a barely perceptible nod.

They were two blocks down the street before Carly's voice, with a forced nonchalance, sounded again from the backseat.

"So, can we get back to this quiz about eye makeup now? Which answer do you choose?"

But Nikki was still wrapped up in her thoughts about all that had just happened.

"I *said*, which—answer—do—you—choose?" Carly's voice came again, and this time her words had a sharper edge. "Nikki? Hel-*lo!*"

Nikki turned partway in the front seat to look at her friend. "Choose? Oh, the quiz," she said. "I don't know, Carly. I can't even remember what the question was."

"Oh, great! How are we ever supposed to get through a 30-day makeover if you can't even stay with me long enough to answer a simple question?" Carly's full lips twisted into an exaggerated frown, and she drew her eyebrows together in an attempt to look stern.

Nikki grinned at her, then felt a familiar pang of envy in the pit of her stomach. Even making faces couldn't do much to damage Carly's incredible looks.

"Sorry, Carly, I was thinking about something else. Read me the question one more time, and I'll listen. I promise," Nikki said.

"What question is this, anyway?" Marta teased. "Number 1,003?"

Carly ignored her. "Okay. Instant replay of the last question in the Eye Makeup IQ part: 'In order to make your eyes appear larger and more noticeable, should you pick an eyeshadow hue that *contrasts with* or *matches with* your natural eye color?' Which one?"

Nikki chewed at her bottom lip, puzzling over the question. Carly sat curled in the backseat in her white shorts and blue Chicago Cubs T-shirt, pencil poised over the blank answer lines on the magazine page.

"I can't remember which one it was supposed to be," Nikki began, but her thoughts went on even after her words stopped. *Even if I got 100 percent on all your beauty quizzes, Carly, I still wouldn't look like you, with your sleek blonde hair and big, brown eyes that grab everybody's attention and . . .*

"What d'you mean, you 'can't remember'?" Carly wailed. "I just read you the answer back on page 32!" She slapped the magazine down against the maroon upholstery and rolled her eyes. "Just explain this to me, Nikki—how can you be such a brain and get all A's in school and not even be able to remember a simple little thing like what color eyeshadow you should use? You know what the problem is with you? You never want to change anything about yourself—"

"Wait a minute," Nikki protested, but Carly cut in with a laugh.

"No, *you* wait a minute, Nikki! Do you know you are absolutely the *only* person I know who still uses blue eyeshadow? Blue eyeshadow has been *out* for an entire year, and you never even noticed! Face it, you're the original stick-in-the-mud. Now listen while I read the answer again!"

Carly snatched up the magazine and flipped to the page

in question. " 'In order to make your eyes appear larger and more noticeable, pick an eyeshadow hue that *contrasts* with your natural eye color.' Got it?"

Nikki nodded. "Got it." She tapped the side of her head with an index finger, dimpling the surface of her shoulder-length dark hair. "It's in here, I promise. I'll consider it my mantra and recite it daily for the rest of my life. Is that good enough for you?"

Marta burst out laughing, but Carly waved her hand to hush Nikki, her lips moving as she added up numbers in the score box at the bottom of the magazine page.

"And," Nikki added, surprised to find she could get a word in, "just for the record, I do *not* get all A's, Carly Allen."

"Yeah, well, close enough," Carly muttered, without looking up from her computations. After another minute, she dropped the pencil in her lap and held up the magazine with a flourish. "Ta-da! Done. Are you guys ready for this?"

"I doubt it," Marta answered. "But something tells we're going to hear it anyway." Then she added, "Better hurry up, Carly. I think we're only about five minutes away."

"Okay, let me remind you that 90 is the highest score you can get," Carly announced. "So, the scores for the Eye Makeup IQ section are: me, 87; Nikki, 43; Marta, 15."

Nikki groaned.

Marta shook her head as she checked her reflection in the rearview mirror. "Sometimes I wonder how I made it all the way into my 30s without you two around to give me advice."

"How many more quizzes did you say are in there, anyway?" Nikki asked, glancing back over her shoulder.

Carly held up the magazine she'd bought the day before at a convenience store in Ohio and pointed to the inch-high red letters on the cover: "The 30-Day Makeover—Raising

Your Beauty IQ from Ho-Hum to Sexy." Underneath, a sub-title promised, "A Quiz for Every Day of the Month."

Nikki groaned again. "Carly! That means we have *28* more to go! How about I just be a beauty dropout, okay?"

"No way." Carly shook her head, blonde hair glistening in the sunshine that flooded the rear window. "You can't be a quitter—I won't let you." Her voice turned coaxing. "Besides, it won't take us 28 days, Nik. It'll only take 14 because we're doing two a day, remember? That way, we can get them done before we go home. And by then, all three of us should be gorgeous. We could even start the next quiz right now." The magazine crackled in her hand as she turned the page and began to read. "It's 'Lipliner, Lipstick, Gloss, or Pencil—Which One's Best for You?' "

"I hate to say it, Carly, but I'm going to be incredibly busy these next two weeks, researching this book. So—" Marta grinned and shrugged her shoulders in mock disappointment "—I guess you'll just have to count me out. I do have this thing called a contract, remember?"

"Oh, great! You're the one who—" Carly broke off in midsentence, but Nikki and Marta finished the sentence in their heads: *needs it most.*

Carly turned toward Nikki. "Well, at least *you* can't bail out on me, Nikki. Besides, it's not all makeup stuff." She leafed through the magazine. "There's stuff on fitness and how to make your personality better and special exercises for thinner thighs and a firmer derriere, whatever that is."

She pronounced it "DARE-e-er," and Marta burst out laughing before she could help herself. "That's 'der-e-*air*,' Carly, and it means your rear end, kiddo."

"Oh. Then why don't they just say so?" Carly laughed with her, then added, "Anyway, you've gotta do this with me, Nikki. I'll never get through the whole makeover thing alone, and I've got *big* changes to make before I go home."

Nikki watched the tree-lined main street of Wald's Ford slide slowly by and pictured all the summers she and Carly had spent on the Lake Michigan shore, Nikki at her grand-parents' and the Allens—Carly's family—in their summer house next door. Carly's makeover project was just a replay of all the other projects she'd wrangled, bribed, and coerced Nikki into over the years.

Nikki had a crystal clear picture of a much younger Carly, standing with hands on hips in front of a gigantic, half-built sand castle, tossing her head so that the long blonde ponytails swung back and forth. "You've *got* to help me, Nikki. There's no way I can do this without you." They'd spent hours finishing the creation, but when two other girls—twins dressed in matching pink bathing suits—stopped to admire their work, Carly had run off to play with them. It was Nikki who got to haul all the sand buckets and shovels and molds back up the steep steps to her grand-parents' house.

And there was just as clear a picture of Carly only two years before, hunched over the desk in Nikki's bedroom at her grandparents', writing furiously on one postcard after another, insisting that Nikki help her or she'd never get enough entries done to win the post-game dinner with Tommy Ditman, right-fielder for her beloved Chicago Cubs.

And of course, Nikki *had* helped, and to everyone's amazement, Carly actually *had* won. Carly got to spend an evening with Tommy Ditman and his wife at Spelante's, which was just about the fanciest and most expensive Ital-ian restaurant in all of Chicago. Nikki got writer's cramp and a book of matches with a picture of Spelante's em-bossed on the cover.

Carly—who was so totally different from her older brother, Jeff, and the younger twins, Adam and Abby—could be absolutely exasperating. But Nikki knew she could

also be a terrific friend. During the past summer and fall,
when Nikki had been pregnant and caught in the toughest
situation she could ever remember, it had been the Allens,
along with her grandparents, who had stood beside her and
helped her through it. And Jeff and Carly had helped most
of all. Nikki shook her head slightly, trying to forestall
thoughts of Jeff—she'd messed up that situation about as
badly as any girl could. But Carly ... well, Nikki owed
Carly a lot.

"All right, Carly, I won't quit, but I still don't get the
point. Why are you so worried about a makeover, anyway?"
Nikki asked. She twisted the heavy, curly dark hair off the
back of her neck and held it up with one hand, hoping that
the air blowing in from the open windows would bring just
a little relief from the stifling summer heat. "I would think
you'd be happy the way you are."

Isn't it enough, Nikki thought, *that every head turns when
you walk into a room?*

Carly began to explain. "School starts in a couple of
weeks, you know, and I have all those new clothes to buy.
That's why I worked most of the summer instead of going
to Lake Michigan like usual." She stopped and shrugged.
"Anyway, Nik, if you have to ask why, you wouldn't understand." She laughed a little, self-consciously. "A girl's
gotta keep up her image, that's all."

Two

MARTA EASED THE TAURUS SLOWLY DOWN Appomatox Street through a neighborhood of tall, two-story wooden houses graced with wide front porches and ornate gingerbread trim, surrounded by long green yards that smelled like they'd been recently mowed. The trees and well-tended flower beds drooped in the heat and humidity of the glaring afternoon sun.

Before long they were passing through the Wald's Ford business district, and Nikki was surprised at how quickly the downtown went by—the whole thing couldn't have been more than two blocks long. It was made up mostly of two-story red brick buildings that housed everything from the General Lee Hotel on the corner—complete with faded confederate flag hung prominently in the lobby window—to Sample's Shoes, where a black, old-fashioned lace-up high heel taller than Nikki herself was fixed permanently to the sidewalk outside the store as an advertisement.

And over the whole town hung the insistent, piercing buzz of cicadas, as though Wald's Ford in August belonged entirely to them.

Marta looked both ways at a stop sign, mainly out of habit, Nikki suspected, considering they hadn't passed another vehicle besides the Rooster's red truck since they entered Wald's Ford, and there wasn't a single one in sight now.

"According to my directions, we're getting close to Dr. Brummels's," Marta said, glancing at the hand-drawn map she was holding, then steering the Taurus through the intersection, "but I know she's not expecting us this early." She glanced at her watch. "I told her we'd be here at 3:00, so we have about an hour to kill. What would you say to a late lunch?"

"Sounds good to me," Nikki agreed enthusiastically. They had driven two hours that morning on mountain roads that gave a whole new meaning to the term "hairpin turns" before stopping at the Virginia state line for a late breakfast of pancakes and sausage. By now the empty, gnawing feeling in Nikki's stomach was back.

"How about you, Carly?" Marta asked. "Ready to eat something?"

Carly hesitated. "If we can find a place that serves salad. Something really light, you know?"

"Well, I'll do my best," Marta said, "but I can't promise. It doesn't look as though Wald's Ford offers too many choices in fine dining."

The houses thinned out quickly, then stopped altogether. There beside a four-lane highway were a gas station and a food stand called Mr. Z's Burgers. They looked down the road beyond. On the right was a farm, and on the left were thick woods crowded close against the roadside.

"I think we just ran out of town," Marta said. "And food options. I'm afraid this will have to do, Carly. And something tells me there hasn't been any radicchio around here in a long time."

Carly groaned, then shrugged at Nikki and Marta with her signature casualness. "Oh, well, guess I'll live."

Marta turned into the empty parking lot, and Nikki opened the car door and swung her stiff legs to the pavement.

"I just hope the bathrooms are decent," Nikki said. "Remember that place we stopped at this morning? Back by the river? Yuk!"

After they finished in the rest room, they stood on the sidewalk and studied the menu board on the wall behind Mr. Z's counter. They could choose between the Tiny Tots burger and fries, the Red-Hot Regular burger and fries, or the Super Southern burger and fries. Cheese, lettuce, and tomato were each a quarter extra.

"Big choice!" Carly muttered, then sighed and stepped up to the counter. "I'll have the kids' thing—I'm not very hungry."

The girl behind the counter, half-hidden behind the screened window, didn't even look up. "You have to be 8 or under to order the kids' special," she said in a bored, sing-song voice.

Carly pursed her lips, and Marta broke in. "Why don't we just get three regulars?"

When the girl put the food on the counter a few minutes later, the burgers were thick and greasy, the fries steaming. They took the food to a picnic table beside the two parking spaces and ate in the shade of the building, swatting at flies and a yellow-jacket that buzzed persistently around them.

"So, Marta," Carly said, squirting ketchup crisscross over her french fries, "how well do you know this Dr. Brummels we're gonna stay with?"

Marta shook her head and swallowed the bite of burger in her mouth. "Not all that well, really. We've been at many of the same conferences, so I've seen her a lot, but I think the first place where we ever actually talked seriously was at the conference in California last April. My publisher had just decided to go ahead with this book on Appalachian folk music, so I asked Dr. Brummels for advice. I was a little nervous about talking to her because of her reputation—everybody had told me that Phyllis Brummels is *the* authority on folk music. But she turned out to be very easy to talk to. She said she's wanted to see a new, updated book on the subject for years."

"So she just invited you to come and stay with her while you worked on it?" Carly asked. "Even though she hardly knew you?"

Marta nodded. "Well, she invited me to stay with her during this Shenandoah Folk Festival we're going to. We got talking, and she said that you couldn't possibly do a book on American folk music and not attend the Shenandoah. Then I found out she's a Christian, too, and all of a sudden it was as though we'd known each other for years. You'll see. She's just a real *comfortable* kind of person. With all her degrees and such, you'd think that she'd be a little unapproachable. I mean, she's been known all around the country for the last 25 years or so for her work in this area, and she travels all over the world and does workshops and lectures—"

"Then why didn't she just write the book herself, since she knows so much about it?" Carly broke in.

Marta took a long drink of her Pepsi. "That's the one thing she was adamant about. She gave concerts, she won piano competitions, and taught at two universities, but she says she draws the line at writing another book. She did one about 30 years ago and swears it was the worst experience of her life." Marta grinned, remembering how emphatic Dr. Brummels had been. "She told me, 'I'll give you all the help and information I can. I'll arrange all the interviews with folk musicians I can. I'll put you up for as long as you want to stay. But you leave me out of the writing part—that's my one condition.' "

They finished their burgers in silence, periodically waving away the yellowjacket, then Marta crunched the grease-stained paper from her hamburger into a loose ball and tossed it into the gray barrel beside the table, sending a small swarm of bees scattering. "So, are you two ready?"

Carly crawled off the bench hurriedly. "Just let me go to the rest room again, okay? I'll be right back."

Nikki giggled. "Carly, you just *went* to the rest room. I swear, you're turning into an old lady with a teeny-weeny bladder."

Carly was already halfway around the side of the white hamburger stand, and she put one hand on her hip and called back over her shoulder, "Just remember, girl, you're a year older than me!"

They watched her disappear behind the bathroom door, and Nikki sighed as she spoke to her aunt.

"It doesn't seem fair, you know? She gets prettier every year. I remember Jeff saying last summer how Carly had really won the 'looks sweepstakes' in their family. I have no idea why this makeover business is so important to her." Nikki frowned, her dark brows pushing the skin over her nose into two vertical lines. "But I've never seen her so . . . so touchy."

She followed her aunt's example and balled up her waxed paper and the red-and-white checked paper boat from her fries. "Oh well, I'm probably being too sensitive. But I really do think she could be a model if she tried, don't you?" She waited a minute for a reply, but none came. "Hey! Earth to Marta," Nikki said. "Are you listening to me?"

Marta's eyes narrowed a little, and she nodded. "Sorry, Nik. I was just trying to picture how Carly looked back at the beginning of the summer, last time I saw her. Seems like she's lost weight since then, doesn't it? It isn't like she *needs* to."

"How could you tell, with those oversized T-shirts she usually wears? Anyway, you know what they say," Nikki answered. " 'You can never be too rich or too thin,' right?" She sighed and added, "Not that *I'll* ever have to worry about either one."

Marta turned to face her, her eyes serious. "You don't really believe that, do you, Nikki?"

Nikki laughed and sipped the last of her soda from the Styrofoam cup, then drew the straw up and down through the plastic lid, listening as it gave a hollow squeal before she answered, "Don't worry, Aunt Marta. It's just one of those things half the country says."

Her aunt watched her skeptically, and Nikki hurried to say more.

"It doesn't mean I actually *believe* it or anything."

Marta lifted one eyebrow. "Really. Well, contrary to half the country, I happen to believe that there *is* such a thing as being too thin." She stood up halfway, bracing her hands on the picnic table and lifting her legs back over the bench until she could straighten up all the way.

Nikki watched her stand, thinking how much her aunt would improve her looks if she dyed her gray-blonde hair back to its earlier shade and wore it down around her shoulders now and then, instead of pulled back haphazardly with the ever-present wooden clip.

Marta's different, though, Nikki thought. *She's too wrapped up in who she's talking to and what she's doing to worry much about herself. Besides, Marta's plain appearance didn't hold Ted back.*

Nikki grinned, thinking back to the old college friend of her aunt's who pastored a small church in Southern

California. Nikki had met him when Marta took her along on a trip there the previous spring. She couldn't resist the chance to tease.

"So, Aunt Marta, you heard from Ted lately?" Nikki asked innocently.

Marta turned and stared at her niece, her lips compressed in a thin, straight line and her eyebrows raised. "Don't—start," she said, emphasizing both words.

Nikki grinned and shrugged, then the bathroom door opened and Carly came out, ending their conversation.

Marta consulted her directions one more time as soon as they got back in the car, then turned the key in the ignition.

As they headed toward Dr. Brummels's house, Nikki took in the view in front of her. There was a gentle quality to Virginia's tree-covered mountains—gentle and relaxed, as though they had nothing to prove. They weren't sharp-peaked and dramatic, like the mountains in California, or majestic, like parts of the Rockies she'd seen. But at high points in the road, Nikki could see range after range of them filling up the miles between her and the horizon, each range a slightly softer shade of blue.

It was easy to lose herself in the beauty of the scene, and she gave a start when Carly's voice sounded from the backseat. "Okay, you guys, the next quiz is—"

Both Marta and Nikki groaned, and Marta spoke. "Sorry, Carly, you're out of time. I think we're here."

As they rounded a bend in the road, she nodded toward the scene ahead. Far out in the center of the valley, at the foot of a tree-covered hill, sat a sprawling house of white clapboard, red brick, and stone. There were fieldstone chimneys at either end of the main section of the house, and a wide porch graced the front of the structure.

It looked to Nikki as though the house had been added on to throughout the years, expanded according to the whims of various owners. With its obvious additions and variety of materials, the house could have looked like a hodgepodge of odd ideas, but it had a homey quality, and Nikki felt welcome there immediately.

Maybe it's the way those big maples come together like a green tunnel over the drive, Nikki thought, *or maybe it's the white wicker furniture on the front porch.* She thought how much different—how much more friendly—it was than her parents' ultramodern brick and glass house in Ohio.

"I'll go see if anyone's home." Marta set off across the gravel turnaround toward the porch steps.

Nikki opened the car door and stepped out. She surveyed the green lawns around her, breathing in the sweet scent of cut grass, and inspected the wildflower bed that took up most of one side lawn. From the porch where Marta was ringing the doorbell came the sound of Westminster chimes. Someone spoke through the screen to Marta, then the squeak of the screen door covered his words.

"What do you think she'll be like?" Carly's voice interrupted Nikki's thoughts.

"What'll *who* be like?" Nikki asked.

"Dr. Brummels, of course. Marta said she's almost 70, didn't she?" Carly bent over and hobbled a few steps as though she were an old lady. Her hand shook violently as she posed it on an imaginary cane, and she sucked in her cheeks and lips as though she had no teeth.

"Carly!" Nikki burst out laughing. "I think you've been shut up in the car too long. Don't be a such a nut."

Carly straightened up to her full five foot five. "Fine, then. Maybe she'll be one of those temperamental musician types, like you." She reached up and wildly ruffled her short blonde hair so that it stood out in all directions from her head and pretended to conduct an orchestra passionately, both hands waving an imaginary baton. Then she stopped and wrinkled her short, straight nose. "Or one of those old ladies who keeps a million cats and forgets to take showers and hoards piles of old newspapers—"

"Or maybe," a low, resonant voice broke in from just behind them, causing Carly and Nikki to whirl around, "she'll turn out to be just your average, everyday type of person, decently clothed and in her right mind."

The owner of the voice put out her free hand and said, "Welcome. I'm Phyllis Brummels."

❦ ✾ Three ✾ ❦

NIKKI WISHED WITH ALL HER HEART that she could disappear into the hard-packed, dry dirt and gravel of the driveway beneath her sandals. She stood silent while Carly stammered a quick apology, but she couldn't help thinking, *This woman doesn't look average or everyday at all.*

The willowy, straight-backed figure before them looked 20 years younger than the age Carly had mentioned. Her hair, still dark and thick with only a few strands of gray, was tied back at the nape of her neck in a green-plaid ribbon that matched her sundress. In her arm, she held a huge bunch of wildflowers from the garden.

"Well, you certainly have some talent as a mimic, I'll say that much," Dr. Brummels remarked dryly when Carly had finished, her voice shaking a little as she spoke. Nikki stared into the woman's dark gray eyes and saw with relief that the trembling was from holding back laughter.

The older woman went on. "From what Marta told me in her letter, I take it you must be Carly?"

Carly nodded nervously, smoothing her hair quickly back into place so that it once again formed its usual sleek, shining frame around her face.

The woman turned toward Nikki. "Which means you must be Nikki, Marta's niece, right?"

"Yes," Nikki said, shaking hands as politely as possible, trying to offset the awkward start they'd made. "Thank you for inviting us to stay with you."

Dr. Brummels smiled. "You're very welcome, but I can't take much credit for my hospitality. I confess I have an ulterior motive. These last two years since I've been semi-retired have been much too quiet, and I'm looking forward to getting involved in Marta's project. Now, why don't we go inside?" She turned toward the porch, calling "Hello, Marta!" as she walked briskly toward the front steps.

Nikki turned to Carly and hissed, "Do you think you could keep from embarrassing us any more? If it's not too much to ask, that is."

Carly pulled her mouth down in an exaggerated frown, and Nikki couldn't keep from laughing. "You're impossible, you know that?" she added.

On the wide front porch, Marta and Dr. Brummels were already deep into conversation about their plans for the next two weeks, and Nikki was surprised to see beyond them in the doorway a boy about her own age. He was still inside, holding the screen door open with one arm, most of his body hidden behind the ornately carved wooden bottom of the door.

As they started inside, Nikki noticed the boy's broad shoulders and the heavily muscled arm that held the door. His hair was brown and unremarkable, as were his eyes, but the warmth of his smile made up for that. It wasn't until Dr. Brummels turned to push the screen door open all the way that Nikki saw the metal crutches supporting his arms at the elbows.

"This is Callan," Dr. Brummels said, introducing him as

though presenting an honored friend or family member. "Callan Forsythe. He's been a voice student of mine for years. His mother lives several miles back in the mountains, so we agreed that for this final year before he goes off to college, he should stay here with me so we can work on his music every day."

Dr. Brummels went on to describe Callan's unusual vocal ability, which included perfect pitch, and added proudly that he'd just been accepted on full scholarship at Eastman School of Music, but it was the boy's left leg that caught Nikki's attention. In sharp contrast to the rest of his body, it was as if there were almost no calf muscle there, nothing but skin sheathing the bone beneath the faded denim cutoffs. She turned her eyes away quickly.

Once Dr. Brummels took hold of the door, Callan turned with difficulty on his crutches and moved back into the entryway to make room for the others. Each movement was accompanied by the metallic click of his crutches, and Nikki was glad when Dr. Brummels's conversation covered the sound.

"Callan, this is Marta Nobles," Phyllis Brummels continued her introductions. "She's a musicologist at Indiana University, and I've already told you about the book she's writing on folk music. And this is Nicole Sheridan, Marta's niece—" she turned to Nikki with her dark eyebrows raised to see if she was getting the information correct "—who will be a senior this year, like you. She's also a very talented musician, Marta tells me, so you two should have a lot in common." Dr. Brummels turned toward Carly and grinned. "And this is Carly Allen, a friend of Marta's family. She's going to be a junior. And, I might add, she is already an *extremely* accomplished mimic."

Carly's creamy cheeks flushed red, but Nikki could see

by the look Dr. Brummels gave her that she was already charmed by the younger girl.

No matter how crazy Carly acts, Nikki thought, *or what kind of dumb stuff she does, people always love her*. She tried to shut out the thought her mind automatically added: *They hardly even notice me.*

Inside, Dr. Brummels's house was as gracious and welcoming as its owner. The rooms had high ceilings and were decorated with a minimum of fuss. When Dr. Brummels pointed out the house's original section, which was well over 200 years old, Nikki found to her surprise that it was the section built of stone, which she had taken for one of the additions.

"This part used to have four small, cramped rooms," Dr. Brummels said as she guided them down the hall, "so I had the dividing walls taken out and made the room into this."

She gestured at the open doorway as they passed, and Nikki could see that the large room, flooded with afternoon sunshine, served as a music studio. Two shiny black grand pianos sat side by side on an oriental rug, lids raised and music racks loaded with open music scores. Callan had followed along with them as far as the studio, and he excused himself now with a slow smile.

"I still have a lot of practice to do today, on Dr. Phyllis's orders," he said.

"Dr. Phyllis?" Carly asked.

"That's me." Dr. Brummels smiled. "Very few people around here address me as Dr. Brummels, since I've lived here most of my life. But they do have great respect for education, so they don't quite want to let go of the 'Dr.' part. Feel free to call me either name—I promise to answer. Come on upstairs with me," she said to Marta and the girls, "and I'll show you where you'll be staying."

They picked up their luggage and followed her up the

wide, polished wooden staircase to the second floor. Marta's room was to the left of the stairs, next to Dr. Brummels's, and Nikki and Carly were directed to the right.

"This is a room I rarely use," the professor explained as she opened the door to the bedroom they would share, "because it's impossible to keep warm in the winter. But I don't expect that will cause you any problem these days. This is a heat wave, even for us."

Carly immediately began checking out the closet and the wide, oval mirror over the old dresser. Nikki crossed the creaky tongue-and-groove floorboards to look out the two ceiling-to-floor windows that took up much of the wall opposite the door. Through the old and faintly wavy glass, she could see the view from the side of the house. Fields spread for a mile or more in front of her, rolling gently, dotted here and there with clusters of trees and a shallow valley where she felt sure a small creek would run. Beyond the little valley, the ground rose to form another steep hill, like the one that created a backdrop to the house.

"The bathroom's right across the hall," Dr. Brummels was saying. "I'm afraid this house was built long before the idea of private baths caught on. If you need anything, just let me know. I'm going to go start dinner. We'll eat in about two hours, and I thought we could discuss Marta's project then and figure out the best way each of us can help her."

Once they were alone, Nikki opened her suitcase and started unpacking. "Well, this shouldn't take long," she told Carly. She jerked hard on the carved wooden handles of a dresser drawer that stuck. "I brought mostly shorts and T-shirts. And a couple of skirts, for church and stuff."

Carly heaved her two bulging suitcases onto the bed with a grunt and unzipped them. Nikki looked at the contents in amazement.

"Why'd you bring all *that*, Carly? We won't even be here two whole weeks."

Carly put her hands to her hips. "What's it matter to you how much I brought?"

Nikki thought at first that Carly was joking, but she stopped short when she saw the look on her friend's face.

"Sorry!" Nikki said. "I didn't mean to upset you—I was just surprised, that's all. I mean, it looks like you brought enough clothes for the whole summer."

Carly turned away and began piling shorts and jeans into the drawers on her side of the big double dresser.

"Well, I happen to be in between sizes, so I had to bring extra stuff." She unfolded a pair of faded blue jeans and held them up to her waist, then shook her head.

Nikki thought of Aunt Marta's earlier comment. "You mean you're *trying* to lose weight?" Nikki asked.

"A little bit," Carly admitted grudgingly.

"But *why?*" Nikki said. "I mean, you're . . . you're just right the way you are now."

Carly shoved a drawer shut, then combed her hair back from her face with her fingers and regarded her reflection in the dresser mirror carefully before she spoke.

"Remember when you were in California last spring? And we were sending E-mail back and forth?"

Nikki nodded and set her cosmetic bag on the top of the dresser.

"Remember how I told you about Jeremy?" Carly continued. "The guy who moved in next door?"

Nikki grinned. "The one you called 'drop-dead gorgeous'?"

"He *is*, Nikki. You wouldn't believe your eyes if you saw him."

"Okay, so what's that got to do with you losing weight?"

Carly shrugged. "Nothing much." She turned back to

her suitcases and grabbed up a pile of lacy, pastel-colored panties and a handful of socks. "Except once, when he was over at our house with Jeff, he made this crack about me having a stomach."

Nikki's eyes widened as she stared at Carly's midsection. "Let me get this straight. You're saying *you* have a stomach?"

"Well, I'm not blind, you know."

Carly turned so she could view herself sideways in the mirror, her hands patting her almost perfectly flat midriff, then glanced back at Nikki, who shook her head in disbelief and opened her mouth to protest. But before she could, Carly changed the subject pointedly.

"So, I thought the weekend with your parents went pretty well."

It was Nikki's turn to feel uneasy. Their two-day stop at her parents' house in Ohio had stirred up feelings she thought had been laid to rest this past year. She was silent for a moment, forming her response.

"Considering you haven't been home for so long, I mean," Carly added. "What'd you think?"

Nikki's thoughts flew back over the last tumultuous year, living with her grandparents in Michigan. She laid the last of her rolled-up socks in the drawer, zipped her suitcase closed, and slid it beneath the bed.

"It went okay, I guess," she said. "I was glad Aunt Marta made time for us to stop there on the way. I mean, actually sitting down and talking to my mother without having a major argument—that was a pretty big achievement."

But she felt stupid as soon as she said the words. Carly would never understand that. How *could* she, with Marlene Allen for a mother? Marlene was the kind of woman who was likely to be named "Mother of the Year" at any time.

"At least she listens to me now," Nikki went on. "Last

year, I could never have told her how I feel about Evan, about giving him up for adoption and all. But she's changed somehow, ever since she wrote me that letter last spring. And this time I felt like . . . like she almost understood, you know? She even asked to see his picture, which is pretty amazing."

Carly began emptying her second suitcase. She set up one bottle after another on the dresser top—astringents and deep-cleansers for her skin, several kinds of lotion and perfume and foundation—until they began to spill over onto Nikki's side. Nikki watched, stopping herself just in time from making a crack about Carly bringing along her own personal pharmacy. A year ago, she wouldn't have thought twice about joking that way, but things were different somehow with Carly these days, and Nikki was treading cautiously.

It wasn't till Carly had lined up the bottles in exact rows—large ones in back, small ones in front—that she spoke again. "Your father wasn't exactly overjoyed to see us."

Nikki shrugged, speaking casually to cover the emotions inside. "Yeah. He seems to be living in his own world these days. He and my mother used to fight a lot, but she says that since I had Evan, they barely speak. He's gone most of the time." She turned and pulled a short terry cloth robe from her suitcase. "Oh well, there's nothing I can do to solve their problems. But I *can* solve one of mine. I'm going to take a shower and get all this sweat off me."

"Don't you mean all that *glow?*" Carly asked, and they both laughed at the reference to Nikki's grandmother, who always told them that ladies didn't *sweat*, they *glowed*. "But wait a few minutes, Nik. We haven't had a chance to talk about Jeff yet." Carly smiled impishly.

Nikki moved toward the door. "Some other time, okay?" She quickly pulled the bedroom door shut behind her but couldn't help hearing Carly's last words.

"You're avoiding the subject!"

Four

BY THE TIME BOTH CARLY AND NIKKI finished showering, changing, and drying their hair, the smell of dinner preparations filled the house. They followed the scent of cooking meat and taco spices down the stairs to the front hall. The rich tones of a baritone voice floated down the hall from the studio where Callan was practicing.

Nikki glanced at Carly, her eyes wide under arched brows. "Wow! No wonder he got a scholarship."

But Carly didn't seem impressed. She turned and walked across the polished hardwood floor toward the smell of food. The kitchen occupied nearly the whole brick addition on the opposite side of the house from the studio. The girls paused in the doorway, and Dr. Phyllis smiled at them over a big basket she was filling with tortilla chips.

"Come on in," she urged. "We were just wondering what was taking you two so long. I have some other friends in here I want you to meet."

They followed her into the kitchen, which had obviously been remodeled recently, with its new white cabinets above the sink. Green-cushioned rockers, each with its own

31

footstool, sat on either side of a wide brick fireplace with a loveseat in between. Next to one of the rockers, which Nikki decided must be Dr. Phyllis's favorite chair, was an end table heaped with mail. The only other furniture in the room was the small rolltop desk pushed against the wall between the kitchen area and the fireplace.

Dr. Phyllis set the basket of chips on the table. "Welcome to the heart of the house," she said, then corrected herself. "On second thought, I suppose the *studio* is the heart of the house, musically speaking. But everything else goes on here. People seem to enjoy being around food—fixing it, smelling it—"

"And eating it!" the smaller of two girls at the counter put in. She lifted her thin, freckled nose in the air with a long, drawn-out sniff of appreciation, then blew a large bubble with her pink gum. The bubble popped with a loud *crack*, and the larger girl beside her sighed.

"Tory," she protested, glancing sideways toward Nikki and Carly as she spoke, "I swear, all you ever think about is eating."

"Well, it may be all I think about, Marissa, but it's all you *do!*" Tory shot back, eyeing the older girl's ample middle. "At least I don't sit around popping my gum and being rude."

Dr. Phyllis sighed and retied the ends of her apron at the back of her plaid sundress. "Carly, Nikki, allow me to introduce the Barkers—Marissa, who's 13, and Tory, who's 11. When not engaged in guerrilla warfare, they happen to be my piano students. They're also neighbors. They live about two miles down the road. Or half a mile over the mountain behind the house, depending on which way you choose to go."

At the professor's introduction, Marissa flushed slightly, her fair skin betraying her uneasiness. She pushed her straight brown hair back from her round face with both hands and sat up on her stool. "Hi. Glad to meet you."

Tory, her brown eyes sparkling, spoke up. "Where are you guys from?" she asked Carly. "How long are you staying?"

"Well, Nik's from Ohio originally, but she's been staying with her grandparents in Michigan for the past year," Carly answered. She straddled the stool beside Tory. "I'm from Chicago, but my family spends the summer at Lake Michigan every year. We have a house there, next to Nik's grandparents', so she and I have kind of grown up together, during the summers at least. And we're here for about a week and a half."

"Do *you* have any sisters?" Tory shot a glance toward Marissa as she spoke, then looked back at Carly. Her tone said clearly, *I commiserate if you do.*

Carly nodded. "One. Abby. She's not much older than you, Tory. But she's part of a matched set—she has a twin, Adam. And then there's my big brother, Jeff. He just graduated from high school." She looked back at Nikki with a wicked grin. "If you want to know more about *him*, you should ask Nikki."

Nikki tried to ignore Carly's words, but she felt her cheeks grow hot. She was glad that Tory's rapid-fire conversation drew all eyes off her.

"Have you seen the kittens?" Tory asked. "They're out in the barn. They'll be six weeks old next Monday, and Dr. Phyllis says we'll be able to take them home then. My dad said we could each have one. I picked the calico one and named it Patches, but Marissa picked the plain old black and white one and named it Boots."

Marissa shifted on the stool, looked down at her hands on the counter, and methodically began cracking her knuckles, one at a time.

"Marissa, you know what Mom says will happen if you keep doing that! Your knuckles will get as big as a truck-driver's." Tory turned back to Carly. "Annie—that's Marissa's best friend—she wanted a kitten, too, but she couldn't have one. Her dad never lets her have anything. Would you like to come out to the barn and see Patches?" She stopped and spoke to Nikki, almost as an afterthought. "You could come, too, if you want." She started to slide off the stool to lead the way, but Dr. Brummels stopped her.

"Not right now, Tory. We're just about to eat. But to-morrow I'll be teaching all morning and Marta will be working on her book, so maybe the girls will be free to see the kittens then."

Tory nodded. "Okay. You know what, Carly? I love your hair." She stretched one of her own brown curls straight out in front of her, then looked back at Carly's blonde hair, which shimmered in the bright ceiling light shining down on them. "Do you play piano, Carly?"

Her conversation changed directions again with the suddenness that kept catching Nikki off guard. *She's like one of those wind-up toys that runs into the furniture, changes directions, and just keeps going.*

"I've been playing for five years," Tory went on. "And Marissa, she started when she was six, too, so she's been playing for seven years. But I'm almost as good as she is. How about you?"

"Me? Play piano?" Carly said. "That's a laugh. Music is Nik's department. She's into music and homework and all that brainy stuff. Personally, I'm more into this." She grasped the bottom of her baggy T-shirt and stretched it down in front of her so that Tory could see the Chicago Cubs logo clearly.

"Baseball?" Tory asked. "You like baseball?"

Carly nodded, grinning at the younger girl, and Tory

returned a happy smile. "Me, too. I *love* baseball."

Only Nikki, standing close to Marissa, heard the little snort of derision that came from the older girl.

Tory gazed at Carly for another moment before asking, "So what do you want to be when you grow up?"

Carly shrugged, then thought for a minute. "I think I'll be a trainer—a personal fitness trainer. A kind of consultant, you know?"

Tory's forehead wrinkled for a minute, then she said with a serious voice, "Me, too. I've always wanted to do something like that."

Marissa blew air through her pursed lips in a loud sigh. "Tory, you've wanted to be a *nurse* ever since you could talk."

Tory waved her sister's comment away with one hand. "You always think you know everything about me, Marissa." She turned her attention back to Carly.

Actually, Tory's more like a little puppy, Nikki thought, *trying to please its new owner.* She glanced at Marissa, who sat slumped over, her elbows on the counter, the fingers of one hand drumming absently on the counter as she watched her sister and Carly. *But Marissa's more like a puppy at the pound that's sure no one will ever want it.*

Nikki heard the metallic click of crutches on the hall floor and realized the baritone singing had stopped some time ago. Callan made his way slowly, deliberately, into the kitchen, glancing around at everyone and grinning.

"Just me alone with six women, huh? I know guys who would kill to be in this situation."

Leaning against the edge of the long table so his hands were free, Callan took silverware and napkins from a stack at the center of the table and set them beside each of the five places, stretching as far as he could without having to move his legs. Marissa went to his side quietly, helping with the place settings that were out of his reach.

"I heard you doing the Schubert, Callan. It was great," she said shyly.

Callan gave her a quick thumbs up and laughed a little at himself. "Thanks, Marissa. I always knew you had a great ear. What's for dinner?"

Dr. Phyllis scraped a meat, cheese, and tomato mixture from the frying pan into a huge glass bowl partially filled with lettuce.

"Taco salad," she answered, "and it's ready right now. Nikki, Carly, could you grab the rolls on the counter there and the juice from the fridge? Marissa and Tory, you'd better get along home or your mother will wonder what happened to you."

Marissa said good-bye politely and went to the door, but Tory backed out slowly, chattering all the while, arranging to visit Carly the next day. They all startled when at last she let the screen door slam behind her with a bang and ran off to catch up with her sister.

Dr. Brummels switched on the ceiling fan over the table before they sat down to eat, then asked Marta to say grace. After she finished, the steaming meat and cheese mixture was passed around. Nikki had a moment of quiet contentment as she watched, waiting for the bowl to reach her.

Through the screen door and open windows came the persistent buzzing of the cicadas, mixed with the scents of honeysuckle blossoms and new hay. Nikki glanced across the table at her aunt and found Marta's eyes on her. Marta winked, and Nikki grinned back. Marta often seemed to read her mind, or at least her feelings, and Nikki knew she was doing so now.

"I suppose we can get down to business," Dr. Phyllis said once everyone was served. "Marta, where would you like to start on this book, and how can we help you? I have plenty of ideas, but I thought I should give you a little room for input here, since it *is* your book." She smiled as she crumbled corn chips across the top of her salad.

Marta chewed thoughtfully for a moment, then answered. "I'm sure just going to the country's biggest and best-known folk music festival will give me all kinds of leads. The publisher wants me to deal mainly with how folk music has changed and evolved, especially over the last 50 years. So what I need from you, Phyllis—besides your going along to the interviews with me, since you know most of these musicians—is information on how the folk music of this area has changed during your lifetime."

Phyllis nodded, listening carefully, and Marta looked at Nikki and Carly. "What I need most from you two is to be extra eyes and ears for me. I'll be busy doing interviews with different musicians while they're here in town to perform, but the one thing this festival is known for is what's called the 'beauty contest.' "

"They have a *beauty contest?*" Nikki said, her mouth still full of meat and tomato. "At a music festival?"

Marta and Phyllis laughed together before Phyllis answered.

"That's just what people around here call it," she replied. "New musicians, the ones who haven't yet made a name for themselves, set up booths around the perimeter of the festival and sing or play their instruments. People walk around and listen to each one, then vote for their favorite new performer. The winner's announced on Sunday night, at the end of the festival."

Phyllis leaned forward, her dark eyes sparkling. "It's the best part of the whole weekend. The people around here love it, because they feel as though the one they've picked may be a famous music star someday. There's sort of a myth that's sprung up around the contest now, because 20 years ago, the president of a big recording studio came through here on vacation and stopped at the festival. He heard one of our own Wald's Ford singers and was so impressed that he offered her a recording contract on the spot. Before that, new musicians came mostly for fun, but since that contract, people have come in droves, with stars in their eyes. Stars that spell Nashville."

"What happened to that singer?" Carly asked. "The one who got the contract? Would we know her name?"

Phyllis shook her head. "I can't even remember it. Her career only lasted about a year, and then she married the president of the recording company and retired. That doesn't stop anyone else, though. They still see this as their big chance."

Marta picked up where Phyllis had left off. "Anyway, what I need you two to do, Nik and Carly, is go around and listen to each new performer. If you hear some who really stand out, you can use my handheld recorder to tape them for me. If the tape sounds promising, I'll go interview them myself. That way, I'll be able to get all my meetings in and still hear the best of the new people."

"You mean you brought us along to *work?*" Carly said, only half joking.

Marta looked at her in surprise. "Carly, I mentioned this in the car. On the way down here, remember?"

Carly shook her head, and Nikki broke in. "Carly, if you would've ever gotten your nose out of that 'Make Yourself Over In 30 Days' magazine or whatever it's called, you'd have heard. But you were too busy giving us beauty quizzes!"

"I could go along, if it would help," Callan put in, his calm voice soothing the awkward moment. Nikki looked at him doubtfully, and he seemed to read her thoughts. "I may slow you down some, but not too much. You mostly just walk a little way between performers, then stand around and listen for a long time."

"That would be excellent," Marta said excitedly. "With everything you know about vocal music, that would be a big help."

They arranged a time to leave for the festival and decided who was riding with whom. The meal was almost over when Marta leaned forward across the table to stare at Carly's taco salad.

"Carly, aren't you hungry?" she asked.

Carly looked down at her plate, which was nearly as full as it had been at the beginning of the meal, minus a few bits of lettuce.

"She doesn't dare eat," Nikki burst out. "She's got to get skinny so Jeremy will fall in love with her!" Nikki grinned at Carly. But to her surprise, Carly looked up at her angrily.

"*Nikki!* You—" Carly began but was distracted when Callan spoke.

"And what's this Jeremy going to change for you?" he asked.

"*Excuse me?*" Carly asked, clearly annoyed at him, too.

"I said, 'What's Jeremy going to change for you?' "

"What would you know about it?" Carly demanded.

"Sorry," Callan said. "I didn't mean to butt in. It just sounded pretty one-sided to me, having to change yourself just to get someone to like you."

Carly glared at him for a minute, then pushed her chair back from the table and spoke pointedly to everyone but Callan, her voice coldly polite. "I think I'll go upstairs and get ready to go to the festival. Would you like me to help clear the table first?"

Dr. Brummels glanced back and forth between Callan and Carly and shook her head. "No, thank you, Carly. This is your first night here, so you're still considered a guest.

Tomorrow, though—that could be a different story. Except for dinner, we're pretty much a self-service operation around here."

Her attempt at lightening things up was lost on Carly, who pivoted on one heel and left the room. Soon they heard her footsteps pounding up the stairs.

Callan sighed. "Well, that's about par for my performance with the opposite sex. Better watch out, Nikki. I'll probably end up sticking both feet in my mouth with you, too, before the day's over."

Nikki regarded his brown eyes, filled with regret, and realized that Carly had scored another conquest in spite of her behavior. "I wouldn't worry too much about it, Callan," she said. "Carly is . . . well, she's just kind of moody these days. I don't think it was really your fault."

Five

THE EARLY EVENING AIR STREAMED soft and warm through the open car window and over Nikki's bare arms as she drove. Sunlight shining through the humidity took on a luminous, golden quality, so that even the closest hills looked mysteriously distant, shimmering in a purple haze that masked trees and buildings.

Nikki braked her aunt's white Taurus at the stop sign and glanced over her shoulder toward Callan while a semi truck roared by on the highway in front of them.

"That's where we had lunch," she told him, nodding across the street to Mr. Z's Burgers. "I didn't expect much, but the food wasn't all that bad."

"Right! If you didn't want anything but greasy burgers and fries," Carly muttered from the seat beside Nikki.

"Hey, don't knock it," Callan said, laughter in his voice. "Mr. Z's is classy dining for Wald's Ford. In fact, if you don't count the restaurant at the General Lee Hotel—which most of us don't—it's our *only* dining, classy or otherwise."

Carly made a small, caustic sound with her tongue, and Nikki frowned. Something about Callan was really bugging

Carly, but there was no way Nikki could bring it up with him right there in the backseat. She checked traffic in both directions, then moved her foot to the accelerator.

The few blocks that made up Wald's Ford went by quickly, and Nikki braked again at the stop sign where the man in the red pickup had confronted them earlier in the day. She noticed once again the bouquet stuck into the chain-link fence. She listened as Callan directed her to turn right toward the county fairground, which lay just beyond the edge of town, then asked him about the flowers.

"Callan? Look at the bouquet stuck in the fence over there. Seems like a weird place to put a bunch of flowers, doesn't it?" Nikki eased the car through the intersection.

"Aha! You've stumbled onto our local mystery," he answered, leaning forward.

"Mystery?" Nikki echoed.

"Yeah. Ever since last spring, someone has put a new bouquet there every few days. And nobody knows who. Or even why—although there was a piece in the Wald's Ford *Gazette* about it a few months ago that gave somebody's theory."

"So what was the theory?" Nikki asked, then interrupted herself when she turned the corner and saw the string of cars stretching several blocks ahead. "You mean I'm supposed to get in line behind all these cars?"

" 'Fraid so," Callan answered, and Carly groaned.

"We'll be here for *hours*," she complained. "There can't be that many people in this whole town."

"The Shenandoah's big doings, you know," Callan answered. "The music's the most important thing, of course, but there's folk art and crafts, and people come from all over to see it. Anyway, the traffic usually moves pretty fast."

"Well, it's not like we have much choice," Nikki said and nosed the car into line behind a green Cherokee. "Aunt

Marta and Dr. Phyllis are probably stuck in this line some-where ahead of us." She put the car into park and leaned back in the driver's seat. "Okay, Callan, back to this the-ory—about the bouquet."

"Right. Last spring, a really bad accident happened there, right at that intersection where the traffic light is. This woman from South Carolina was on her way home from visiting her parents up in Maryland, and both she and her baby got hurt really badly. The mother's still in a coma, last I heard. The other car was driven by a guy from here in Wald's Ford, a guy who drinks a lot, but the police really messed up. They didn't get around to testing him for al-cohol for hours, and they could never prove whether he was drunk or not when it happened. He got off on some kind of technicality. About a week later, flowers started showing up, stuck into that chain-link fence, and the theory is that somebody's putting them there in memory of the accident. Or to say they're sorry. Something like that."

Nikki shifted the car into drive and let it glide forward, her eyes on the bumper of the Cherokee. "Somebody's been doing that all these months? Leaving flowers?"

"Yeah, every week or so. And nobody knows who. Or, if they do, they're not talking."

They waited in line for at least 20 minutes until it was their turn to park. When at last a stocky, gray-haired man with a Day-Glo orange vest and Lions Club T-shirt waved them across the bumpy field that served as an overflow parking lot and directed them to an empty space, Nikki turned off the ignition. Callan braced himself with one hand against his open doorway, then reached back inside to grab his metal crutches. Once he fitted them in place beneath his elbows, he pushed the car door shut and straightened up. He noticed both Nikki and Carly watching him.

"Hey, like I told you, I won't hold you up. Not much, anyway."

His grin was relaxed, and Nikki smiled back, her tension broken by his straightforward attitude. Carly, though, seemed uneasy, concentrating on locking the car door and surveying her reflection in the window. She fussed with her bangs, though they were already in perfect order.

"Come on, let's get going," she said. "It's taking hours just to *get* there."

The Shenandoah Folk Festival sprawled across the entire Mountain County Fairgrounds and overflowed onto the streets around it. People seemed to be everywhere—and so did the greasy smell of fried funnel cakes and cheese nachos. But it was the noise that hit Nikki most of all, with sound spilling from every corner of the fairgrounds.

An electronic voice, distorted with amplification, drifted from the large building in the center of the fairgrounds. Mixed with that were the voices of hundreds of festival-goers milling about in the warm summer evening, making their way in the same direction as Nikki, Carly, and Callan. And through it all came the sounds of singers and instrumentalists performing, each in small roped-off areas spaced a few hundred feet apart around the edge of the fairgrounds.

The sounds blended together in a bewildering cacophony, and Nikki wondered how they'd ever be able to distinguish one performer's music from the others'. But when they finally stopped in front of one roped-off area, where a man wielded small sticks over a hammered dulcimer, she noticed how the sweet, bell-like tones of his instrument shut out the sounds of the other musicians.

"Andy Allender," Nikki read the sign over his roped-off area, "Battleboro, Vermont." She turned to Callan and asked, "Vermont? That's a long way to come for a music festival."

Callan straightened up slightly from leaning on his crutches, rolled his eyes, and grinned. "You're pretty determined, aren't you?"

"Determined?" Nikki asked, confused. "What d'you mean?"

When he answered, Callan spoke in an exaggerated Southern drawl. "Determined to convince yourself this here's just a little ol' hick town with just a little ol' hick music festival."

"I am not—" Nikki began, but he cut her off, his voice back to normal.

"I keep telling you, Nikki, this is the single biggest folk festival in the country. People come here from all over." He turned to Carly with a glint in his brown eyes and spoke as though they were allies. "Tell me, is she always this hard to convince?"

But Carly barely acknowledged his question, and Nikki watched a little of the sparkle go out of his eyes. Nikki wanted to reach out and give Carly a good shaking.

What would make her be so rude to Callan? Nikki wondered. *His one simple comment at dinnertime about changing herself for someone else? That makes no sense at all.*

When Callan spoke again, his voice startled her out of her thoughts. "Don't like Andy Allender, huh?"

"Why do you say that?" she asked.

"Because of the look on your face," he answered, and Nikki realized she'd been frowning.

"No." She laughed at herself for getting so deeply lost in her thoughts. "No, actually I think he's really good."

On the little wooden stage, the musician, clad in a gray T-shirt and jeans, leaned intently over the hammered dulcimer. His hands flew so fast that they moved in a blur, the sticks striking the strings of the instrument with perfect accuracy. The sound of the dulcimer cascaded around her.

"He's incredible, actually," Nikki said. "I can't imagine learning to play an instrument like that."

"But you play piano, you said," Callan answered.

"Well, sure, but that's different. I mean, you get to know where you are on the keyboard by the way the white and black keys are grouped. But I can't see anything on his instrument but a bunch of strings, and they all look the same to me."

Carly spoke up then, looking at Nikki. "Have you seen enough of this one? I'd like to hear some of the singers, because I can't even tell what song this guy's playing."

The three of them moved on together, shouldering their way through the tightly packed groups around each performer. Nikki found herself walking slightly ahead of Callan, opening a path for him as he maneuvered his crutches over the uneven ground.

Down the path from Andy Allender was a group called the Mountainaires, dressed in matching western-style plaid shirts, tight jeans, and ornate, pointed-toe boots with two-inch heels. The man in front picked out a melody on his banjo with lightning precision while the rest of the group behind him fiddled with great gusto. The crowd around this roped-off area was clapping and hollering, laughing out loud as the man's fingers flew.

"Well," Callan said, leaning toward Nikki so she could hear, "sometimes we blur the line between folk and country music around here. I admit it."

A few couples near the back of the group were dancing to the music, the men whirling the women around in a square dance routine, and Nikki found after a minute or two that her own foot was tapping and her head nodding in time.

Callan took in her moving foot and head and snapped his fingers as though he'd just missed a big chance.

"I'd ask you for this dance, but I'm afraid you'd get your toes trampled by four feet that way, not just two." He nodded toward the rubber-tipped ends of his metal crutches, then lowered his voice so Carly couldn't hear. "Don't think I'd better ask her, though."

Nikki answered just as quietly. "I'm sorry, Callan. I don't know what's bothering her. I've never seen her act this way."

Callan flexed his shoulders up and back in a circle, and Nikki thought how tense his arms must become, leaning on crutches that way. Then he shrugged. "Hey, it's not your fault. Don't worry about it."

After the Mountainaires, they watched two nearly identical acts. Each woman performer had a huge head of long, elaborately curled hair and tons of makeup, each of them a carbon copy of a famous country singer currently on the charts.

Callan stopped in front of the second booth and raised one eyebrow. "Original, huh? We always get a few wannabes here, if you know what I mean. You have to take some of these acts with a grain of salt, but if you keep looking, you usually find a couple that are really worth hearing."

They walked and listened for at least an hour as darkness crept across the fairgrounds, the long summer twilight lingering over purple mountains beyond. Nikki thought how pleasant the soft warmth of the summer evening felt against her bare shoulders and legs, and how many memories of county fairs and childhood carnivals it brought back. The bright lights, the noise of the crowds and smell of hot dogs and nachos from the vendors' carts were so familiar that she almost expected to turn a corner and come upon a Ferris wheel gliding silently around and around.

A moment later, Nikki was snapped out of her reverie

as she and Carly and Callan came to the next roped-off performance area. Singing there was a girl with the most
incredible voice Nikki had ever heard. She was a thin, plain-
looking girl—a child, really, Nikki thought—dressed in a T-
shirt and miniskirt, sitting on a wooden stool with one foot
twisted around its legs as though to hold herself in place.
She cradled her guitar against her and strummed it almost
absently, her attention focused on the plaintive words of the
old folk song she sang, her eyes fixed on a point above the
heads of the crowd gathered in front of her. Unfortunately,
someone had made up her face badly, using far too much
hot-pink blush and green eyeshadow. Still, unlike the previous two singers, this girl made no attempt to capture the
crowd's attention.

Nikki listened to the girl sing, "He's gone away, 10 million miles . . . And who will tie my shoes? And who will
kiss my ruby lips?"

Both Nikki and Callan stood perfectly still, arrested by
the round, full tones that seemed to float without effort from
the girl's small body and hang suspended in the soft evening air.

"I know her," Callan whispered to no one in particular.

Carly stumbled to a stop behind them, bumping into
Nikki. "Hey! How come we're stopping at this one?" she
asked.

Nikki knew that in Carly's eyes, this girl would be just
one more singer. One that needed a makeover, at that.

Carly looked at the singer and her eyes narrowed. Nikki
could almost hear her thinking: *I'd get rid of all that hot-pink
blush, use a good layer of ivory beige foundation to cover all those
freckles—blue-based to correct the yellow tones in her skin—then
some good mascara to make those sandy-colored lashes a lot darker.*
Carly tilted her head to one side as she watched, combing
her hair back from her face with the fingers of one hand.

Nikki was sure she was thinking, *And that red hair, curling halfway down her back—that'd have to go, for sure. A good, short cut for body* . . .

Callan motioned toward Marta's tiny tape recorder that Nikki had been carrying, unused all this time, and she moved as close as she could to the singer and pressed "record" for the first time that evening.

A minute later, the song ended on a plaintive note, and Nikki suddenly felt that she was beginning to understand the whole idea of folk music. Up till now, this had been just Marta's project, and helping out was simply a ticket for her to go along on a two-week trip to a part of the country she'd never seen. But now, Nikki could hardly wait to share the recording with her aunt.

Sliding off the stool, the singer grasped her guitar by the neck. As she turned toward the small tent enclosure at the back of the roped-off area, shouts of "Encore! Encore!" rose above the burst of applause. She seemed unsure what to do. She nodded back at the crowd and smiled, a slightly lopsided smile that communicated more confusion than happiness, and disappeared through the tent door.

"Wow!" Callan said, his mouth close to Nikki's ear so she could hear over the clapping and shouting. "I had no idea Annie could sing like that. This has got to be one of the best-kept secrets in town. Maybe in the state."

"How do you know her?" Nikki asked.

"That's Annie Slayton, Marissa's friend. Marissa's always telling me Annie can sing, but to be honest, I didn't pay much attention. She's probably going into high school this year." He paused a moment, then nodded. "Yeah, I'm pretty sure she's a freshman, a year ahead of Marissa. It's just that she's the kind of kid who fades into the wallpaper, you know, but you'll definitely want to let your aunt hear this tape."

Callan shifted on his crutches and opened his mouth to continue, but Carly cut in before he could.

"Do you have any money with you, Nik?" she asked. "I've been smelling those funnel cakes for over an hour now, and I can't stand it anymore."

But Nikki was hoping Annie would reappear and do another song. She waited, hushing Carly, until nearly everyone else drifted away.

"Let's go talk to her, Callan," she said. "I think this is just the kind of thing Marta's looking for. Come on."

Nikki and Callan started toward the tent, and Carly fell in step behind them with a groan and muttered something about "funnel cakes," but a loud voice from behind the tent flap made all three of them stop dead in their tracks just outside the doorway.

"You mind what you say to me! You might be out there acting like the big star, but don't you go gettin' too big for your britches with me, young lady!"

There was a muffled reply, a girl's voice saying words Nikki couldn't quite make out.

"Oh, is that right? Well, if you'd do what I tell you and put yourself into your singin' like those other gals, you'd be bringing in some money 'stead of just fooling around with that guitar, wasting time. D'you see that one in the booth next to us there? The one who knows how to move to the music some? Shoot, next to her you look about as interesting as a blank screen on a TV. And I'm tellin' you again—you need to get you another name, a stage name. Something folks'll remember."

"Annie was my *mother's* name, and I'm not changing it!" This time the girl's voice was defiant and easy to hear.

"Listen, girl, you're gonna do what *I* say, hear? You're gonna change it. Period. I'll think of somethin' catchy, like . . . Lola. Or . . . I don't know, Darla."

"Why, Daddy? So you can forget *everything* about Mom? Not just the way she always begged you to stop drinking, but even her *name?*"

There was a crash from inside the tent, as though something large had hit the ground, and the tent flap snapped open. Silhouetted in the light of the doorway was a short man in boots, jeans, and a T-shirt. Nikki started in surprise, and Carly drew back with a little gasp. It was the man who had reminded Nikki of a rooster, the man Carly had yelled at.

But he was far too enraged to notice them. He turned to look back inside the tent, and his voice roared. "Don't you ever, *ever* talk to me that way again, girl! You hear me?"

Then he strode off down the path, his boots crunching on the gravel. From inside the tent came the sound of sniffling.

When he disappeared, Nikki moved closer. Through the open tent flap, she could see Annie on her knees, gathering up pages of sheet music that had spilled out of a broken crate on the ground.

Nikki remembered the man's words to her aunt at the stop sign that afternoon and thought, *I guess we know now what he'd do if he ever heard his girl sass.*

She started to move nearer, but Carly grabbed her arm. "Let's get out of here!" she whispered.

"But she needs help," Nikki hissed back.

"Which is exactly what we're going to need if her crazy father comes back and recognizes me. Come *on!*" Carly pulled at her arm insistently.

Callan watched them both curiously, but he didn't ask any questions until they were standing at the counter of one of the food booths. Nikki watched the gray-haired booth attendant fish out three funnel cakes from a frying vat with a slotted spatula. He shook a tarnished metal shaker of confectioner's sugar over them so that a thick drift of white covered each one. The cakes were crisp on the outside, a delicate brown from their brief float in the hot fat.

"So what was all that about back there?" Callan asked them. "Why would Annie Slayton's father recognize you?"

Carly rolled her eyes. "It'll take too long to explain."

"It will not," Nikki said, laughing. "You just don't want Callan to know what you did." She turned to him. "Carly tried to give Annie's father a little advice on how to drive today, back at that stop sign where the flowers were. In fact, she yelled it at him out the car window, and believe me, it didn't go over well at all."

Callan's eyes widened. "You yelled at *Leonard Slayton?* And lived to tell about it? I'm impressed."

"Oh, come off it. Nikki's just making a big deal out of nothing. Mmmm." Carly changed the subject with an exaggerated sigh of appreciation, her eyes closed as she bit into her funnel cake. "This is absolutely my favorite food in the whole entire world."

"I thought that honor belonged to spaghetti," Nikki said.

Carly shrugged and grinned. "That, too," she answered, but her mouth was so full of funnel cake that her words came out "Thad, doo," and they all burst out laughing.

They paid for the cakes and left the foodstand, settling at a nearby picnic table, Carly perched on the corner, engrossed in her cake. A breeze came up, bringing with it the smell of cut hay from fields beyond the fairgrounds and blowing their napkins off the table and into the darkness. Callan went to get more, and Nikki took her chance.

"Carly, why don't you like Callan?" she asked. "He's a really sweet guy."

Carly shrugged and unwound a long strip of fried dough, white with confectioner's sugar.

"C'mon, Carly, why don't you like him?" Nikki

persisted. "It isn't because he's . . . he's handicapped, is it?"

Carly looked up, her eyes clouded with anger. "Oh, right, Nik. Now I'm a bigot. Down on the handicapped. Thanks a lot!"

"Okay, then, what is it? You tell me."

"Nikki, use your head. The guy's got the brains of a bagel. He annoys me, all right?"

Before they could say anything else, Callan came back with more napkins, and Nikki noted the relief that showed on his face as he sank to the bench and leaned his crutches against the seat beside him. She resolved to be more aware of the effort it cost him to trek around the huge fairgrounds with crutches and purposely began a conversation so he'd have extra time to sit.

"Tell me how you ended up staying at Dr. Brummels's," she said.

With the back of one hand, Callan brushed away the powdered sugar that frosted his upper lip. "That's just the way she is," he said, shaking his head slowly back and forth as he spoke. "She looks at you, figures out what you need, and then convinces you that you'd be doing *her* a favor if you let her give it to you."

Carly's eyes narrowed at Callan. "Excuse me, but that last sentence didn't make a lot of sense."

Callan laughed. "You're right, Carly. I guess you just have to know Dr. Phyllis." He shifted his weight on the wooden bench. "I started taking piano lessons from her when I was six, and one day she told me to sing a line of music I couldn't play. From the minute she heard me sing, I never stood a chance. She went home with me that day, convinced my mother that *she* would be lucky to have *me* as a student, and the next thing I knew, I was having both piano and voice lessons, at no extra cost because she knew my mother could barely afford the money she was already paying."

"But I still don't understand how you ended up staying at her house," Nikki said.

Callan watched a june bug lumber across the rough wooden slats of the picnic table in the bright path of light from the vapor lamp high overhead. When he spoke, his voice was quiet.

"My dad left when I was six, and there's never been a whole lot of money around our house." The bug reached the crumpled napkin Callan had dropped on the table, and it stopped, its feelers waving up and down. Callan brushed the napkin aside, and the shiny beetle lumbered on its way again.

"We live about 15 miles on the other side of Wald's Ford, and it took a lot of time for my mother to drive me in for lessons twice a week. She's a waitress down in Lima—that's about 20 miles on the other side of our house. So Dr. Phyllis suggested she'd really like to have someone else around the house now that she's sort of retired and asked if I'd consider staying there this year." He looked across the table at Nikki and grinned. "Like I'm doing her some kind of favor."

Nikki was about to ask another question, but Carly swung herself off the corner of the table in one easy, graceful movement. She balled up her napkin and waxed paper and shot them at the blue plastic barrel that served as a trash can.

"Two points," she said, then reassessed her distance from the target. "On second thought, I'll give that one three. I'm gonna go find the rest room. You guys'll wait here, right?"

"I'll come with you," Nikki began, but Carly waved her back.

"I think I can handle it myself," she called over her shoulder, brushing her hands together to get rid of the powdered sugar as she strode away.

Six

ON SATURDAY MORNING, NIKKI finished her shower, wrapped her wet hair in a fluffy white bath towel, and pulled her terry cloth robe close around her. She'd suddenly gotten the idea, as hot water and shampoo suds cascaded down over her shoulders, that since Carly had been a Christian so much longer than she had, they could have devotions together on this trip. Nikki knew that would solve whatever the strain was that seemed to be growing between them.

Maybe we could even pray together. I could sure use some help in that department, she thought.

She hurried across the hall, pushed open the door, and started to speak, but Carly's actions stopped her dead.

Carly was sitting on the floor, halfway through a sit-up on the throw rug beside her bed. She startled as the door opened and, with a fast sweep of her arm, shoved something under the bed. Then she sat all the way up and began to chatter quickly, combing her fingers through her hair as she spoke.

"Hey, Nik! I'm up to 100 sit-ups now. And 40 leg lifts.

What do you think of *that?* You should be doing these with me, you know."

Nikki frowned and unwound the towel from her head. Dark, wet hair fell down around her face, the ends already beginning to curl.

"Carly, you're exercising again? Don't I remember you waking me up at seven this morning, scrounging around in the closet for your running shoes? And weren't you gone for an hour or more, jogging?"

"So what?" Carly snapped, instantly defensive. "I had a great run. But a person's got to do more than that—running won't get rid of a stomach, you know that. Anyway, it's *my* business how much I exercise."

"But why are you doing all this? I don't understand."

Carly spread both hands out to her sides, palms up. "I've told you and told you, Nik, but you just don't listen. I have to lose five more pounds. It's that simple—I *have* to."

"Carly, you're *nuts* if you think you need to lose any more weight," Nikki said in frustration. "Would you just look in the mirror and see reality? You're—"

But Carly, her face flushed, gave Nikki no chance to go on. She sprang to her feet, grabbed her robe off the bed, and started for the door. "And right now, I have to take a shower."

Nikki stared after her for a moment, still frowning, then got down on her knees and peered underneath Carly's bed. It took her eyes a second to adjust to the darkness, but she could smell what Carly had hidden before she could see it.

Even then, it didn't make any sense.

Potato chips? Nikki pushed the super-sized bag aside and spotted a white, rectangular box behind it. She reached as far as she could and grabbed the box, pulling it forward so she could see inside the cellophane top. Chocolate donuts?

The frown lines between Nikki's eyebrows deepened,

and she sank back on the rug, arms wrapped around her knees, trying to put together what could be going on with Carly. Her irritability, her rudeness to Callan, her dogged determination to get rid of a nearly nonexistent "stomach." But every trail Nikki's mind followed stopped in a dead end. None of it made sense. It was like opening a book written in French and trying to read it—with her three years of Spanish.

Unless . . .

Things she'd heard in school and seen on TV about situations like this came flooding back into her mind. *But no,* Nikki pushed the thoughts away. Carly would never get involved in something like that. She just wasn't the type.

Of the three friends—Carly and Jeff Allen and Nikki— Carly had been by far the most open and easygoing, always ready to have a good time. Nikki couldn't help grinning as she remembered the day Carly had painstakingly removed the cream filling from an entire plate of Twinkies and refilled them with mayonnaise, just to see the expression on her family's faces when they bit into the treats. Or the night Carly slept over and they couldn't find anything to do. She could still see Carly experimenting with how many minimarshmallows she could pack in her nose, then sneezing them out. They'd both laughed till they rolled on the floor after that one. Carly had an almost photographic memory for jokes and could tell them by the hour until she had Nikki close to being sick from laughing.

Carly had *always* been fun. Until now.

Now everything was so serious. The constant exercise didn't seem so much like something Carly *wanted* to do as much as something she *had* to do. And the makeover thing—even something like that, which should have been good for a lot of laughs, was serious business now to Carly.

So what's going on with her? She's never been moody. At least, she was always a lot less moody than I am, that's for sure, Nikki thought. But now, Carly seemed like a different person.

Even more confusing, the change wasn't consistent. Just when Nikki thought she was getting used to the new, moody Carly, the old one with the impish grin and outrageous sense of humor popped back up. But just when Nikki went to welcome her old friend back with open arms, Carly turned into a stranger who lost her temper for no reason.

I need to talk to Aunt Marta, tell her what's going on here. I think Carly's in some kind of real trouble. But another part of her answered back, *How? How can you tell Marta something you can't even put into words?*

She leaned her head against her knees. *You know, Lord, sometimes it seems like You're the only one in my life who stays the same. But even though she's changed so much, Carly's been one of my best friends for as long as I can remember.*

And I miss her.

From across the hall, Nikki heard the squeak of the shower faucet being turned off. She quickly shoved the donuts and chips back where she'd found them and hurried to grab her blow dryer from the top dresser drawer. She had the diffuser in place and was bent over double, blowing the back of her long hair forward before Carly opened the bedroom door.

By the time the girls finished dressing and went downstairs, Aunt Marta and Dr. Phyllis were already at the breakfast table, laughing as Callan recounted his morning trip to the barn to feed the kittens.

"Something smells great in here," Nikki said after she greeted the others and settled in a chair, scooting it closer to the table. "What's for breakfast?"

Carly was just bending to sit down as Dr. Phyllis announced, "Eggs, fried country ham, grits, and red-eye gravy."

Carly stopped. She wrinkled her nose, then glanced across the table and rolled her eyes at Nikki. "Eggs and ham—that's good. But what are *grits?*"

Dr. Phyllis laughed out loud. "You've never had grits? Oh, Carly, are you in for a treat." She reached out to pick up the covered white, oval dish in front of her. She set it in front of Carly and removed the lid with a flourish. "*This* is grits. Steaming hot, ready for a nice, fat pat of butter and some red-eye gravy. We are talking Southern-style breakfast here."

Carly leaned forward and sniffed suspiciously. "That still doesn't tell me what these things are. I mean, they're white like rice, but they're too small to be . . . "

She broke off as Callan shook his head back and forth and snickered softly.

"What?" she asked. When he did not answer, Carly questioned him again, this time more indignantly. "*What, Callan?*"

Callan went on shaking his head, looking down at his own plate heaped with grits. "My mother told me Yankees were like this, but I never believed her. Guess I should've listened."

Carly's brown eyes narrowed as she frowned at Callan, and Nikki bit her lip. *Be careful, Callan,* she thought. *She blows up without warning these days.*

But before Carly could say anything, Dr. Phyllis spoke, playing along.

"Didn't I always tell you to pay more attention to your mother, Callan?"

"Yes'm," he answered with an exaggerated Southern drawl. "And here you were right all the time." He turned toward Nikki and Carly. "Mama always told me you could tell a true Yankee because he referred to grits as *they* and *those*, but I never did believe her. Any Southerner worth his salt knows that grits is *singular*."

"What are you talking about?" Carly snapped.

"It's very simple," Callan said with mock seriousness. "Do you say 'those oatmeal'? Do you say 'those cornmeal'? Of course not. Now listen up and I'll teach you a little bit about being Southern. Repeat after me: 'I love grits. Grits *is* great. I eat *it*—not *them*—every chance I get.'"

"I'm not saying any such—" Carly began, but Callan's head snapped up, his eyes sparkling as though he'd just had a brilliant idea. He talked right over her.

"You know what I think?" he said to Phyllis. "I think we ought to educate Carly about Southern cuisine while she's here." He laid his fork across the top of his plate and grinned. "I mean, we could have a different Southern delicacy every day she's here. By the time she leaves, she could be one really smart Yankee."

Phyllis joined in, straight-faced. "Excellent idea, Callan. We could have liver pudding!"

"Boiled pigs' feet," Callan shot back.

Carly groaned.

"Chitlins," Phyllis said.

"Or cracklins."

"I know!" Phyllis said. "We could have an old-fashioned pozole, the kind where you use lye hominy and a real hog's head and—"

Carly put both hands on her stomach. "This is absolutely the *grossest* conversation I've ever heard. I give up!" But she was smiling, and Nikki sighed with relief that Carly had finally relaxed enough to see she was just being teased.

Carly put out her hands to take the dish. "So I'll eat some grits, okay? I'm sure they're delic—"

"Uh, uh, uh!" Callan wagged his finger back and forth at her.

"I'm sure *it's* delicious!" Carly said and spooned a tiny

bit onto her plate, then into her mouth and swallowed. "There. Now is everybody satisfied?"

They all laughed at the surprised look on Carly's face as the taste caught up with her.

"You know what? They're not . . . I mean, *it's* not all that bad. Kind of buttery tasting."

"Well, there's a reason for that," Marta said, laughing. "I watched Phyllis fix it, and I think she used a whole cup of butter."

"Naturally," Phyllis declared. "That's one of our deep, dark Southern secrets. Nobody really eats grits for the grits itself—they eat it for the butter. Seriously, though, I think Callan's idea is a great one, in moderation. I'll try to plan some real Southern meals for the three of you while you're here, though I'll probably skip the liver pudding."

She went on, but Nikki wasn't listening. Her attention was focused on Carly's face. As soon as Marta mentioned the butter, Carly's nose wrinkled, and she licked her lips as though she'd eaten something foul.

The teasing around the table went on, but Carly was no longer laughing. Within a minute or two, she excused herself, and Nikki could tell from the creaking of the floor overhead that she'd gone back upstairs.

Marta pushed her chair back from the table. "Well, I've got your tape from the festival to listen to, Nikki, and a lot of notes from last night's interviews to get typed up. Time to spend a few hours bonding with my laptop."

"So, do you think you could get one for me at the store?" Dr. Phyllis asked, and from the volume of her voice, Nikki knew it wasn't the first time she'd asked.

Nikki looked up, confused, and realized she had no idea what Dr. Brummels was talking about.

"I'm sorry, Dr. Phyllis. I guess I wasn't listening. I

was . . ." She trailed off with a shrug, wishing she could just tell the truth and say, *I was listening for Carly's footsteps, wondering why she was in such a hurry to go back upstairs.*

Callan smiled his gentle, teasing smile at her from across the plate of pink ham slices and raised his eyebrows.

"Not only do Yankees have trouble appreciating good food, they have short attention spans, too, huh?"

"Maybe that's true," Nikki said, laughing. "For me, anyway."

Phyllis gathered her napkin together in a loose fold and laid it beside her plate. "As I was saying, I found out last night that today is Marta's birthday. I know she loves Boston cream pie, and I thought perhaps you and Carly could pick one up at the store for me. I'd much rather bake one for her myself, but I have to teach all morning and most of the afternoon. I can manage a decent dinner, but I know I won't have time to bake."

"Sure," Nikki answered. "We can do that. Just give me directions to the bakery." *And I can get a card and present while we're in town, too,* she thought, guilty that she'd completely forgotten her aunt's birthday.

Carly was still in the bathroom when Nikki went back upstairs. Nikki waited in the bedroom for her long enough to pick up her nightshirt and robe and hang them on the hook in the closet, then sort through the neatly aligned bottles of fingernail polish on Carly's side of the dresser, trying to find a color she liked. When she picked up the bottle labeled Shimmering Mauve, several bottles fell around it like dominoes, and Carly picked that precise moment to push open the bedroom door.

"Nik, what're you doing with my stuff?" she demanded.

"I was just gonna do my nails. You were in the bathroom so long, I figured I may as well get something useful done."

Carly shut the door behind her and put a hand on her hip. "Well, you may not have noticed, or cared, but I had all my stuff in a certain order." She crossed to the dresser beside Nikki and began to straighten the little bottles of polish. "If it's not too much trouble, how about asking first next time?"

Nikki gave a little snort of disbelief. "Carly! We've been using each other's stuff for years without asking. I mean, how many hundreds—no, *thousands*—of times have you worn my earrings? And perfume? And—"

"Forget it, Nikki. You just don't understand."

That's an understatement, Nikki thought, watching Carly's hands move with sharp, angry motions as she restored her side of the dresser to its unnatural order. *How can Carly, who's never had less than three days worth of clothes thrown haphazardly over the end of her bed at one time, have suddenly become a neat freak?* She puzzled silently for a few minutes, then tried to begin again in a casual tone of voice.

"Look, Carly, I forgot all about this, but today is Aunt Marta's birthday. Dr. Phyllis wants us to go into town and get her a cake. And I need to find a card and some kind of present. Want to go with me?"

Carly carefully balanced the last bottle in its place, then turned around with a smile. "Sure. When do you want to leave?"

Nikki, taken aback by the sudden change of mood, hesitated for a second. "Well, right now, I guess."

"Fine," Carly said. "Let me get my shoes on, and I'll be ready."

"Okay," Nikki said, shaking her head back and forth. "I'll go get the car."

It was as though there had been no conflict between them. On the drive into town, Carly chattered endlessly, and Nikki was glad to hear her sound so much like her old self again—at least until she brought up the subject of her brother, Jeff.

"Did you know I called home last night?" Carly asked.

"Uh-huh," Nikki said, stopping for a car that was trying to parallel park in front of them.

"I talked to Jeff."

"Really?" Nikki answered, careful to sound nonchalant.

"Yeah, he said to be sure and tell you 'hi.' "

There was silence for a minute, then Nikki said, "Well, tell him I said 'hi' back, okay?"

More silence filled the car, then Carly burst out, "Nik, what happened between you two? Jeff really liked you! I mean, last summer and fall, you were practically the only thing he could talk about. Then, right after you had the baby, something changed. He won't talk about it, and neither will you."

Checking over her shoulder and pulling out to pass the car ahead, Nikki took a deep breath and let it out in a slow, controlled stream.

"I'm not really sure exactly what happened, Carly," she answered, though her conscience started up instantly.

That's not the whole truth, is it? You blew it with Jeff. Admit it, Nikki. He kept reaching out to you, trying to be there for you. He even told you about the Lord. Where would you be now if he hadn't? But you just kept pushing him away, time after time.

She thought back to the night last winter when Jeff tried to keep her from going out with Chad, who had so obviously been drinking. *But did you listen, Nikki? Oh, no. You had to go and get mad and shoot off your mouth. Not just once, either. And then, by the time you finally came to your senses and realized what a great guy Jeff really is, it was too late.*

Too late. Regret washed over her at the echo of the words in her head, regret and memories all jumbled together. She could still hear his voice: *"You'll be glad to know,*

Nik," he'd said, sitting in front of the fire at his house that night, *"that I've decided I'm gonna just kind of get on with my own life ... quit bugging you.... I hope we'll always stay friends ..."* Could there be any words that closed their relationship more finally than those?

Friends. That was the moment when she'd realized just how desperately she wanted Jeff to be more than a friend. But by then it was too late.

Carly reached over and punched Nikki lightly on the upper arm. "Hel-*lo*. Earth to Nikki! I don't think you've heard a word I've said for the last five minutes. How about coming back from wherever you are?"

"Sorry," Nikki said. "Guess I checked out on you for a minute there. What'd you say?"

"I was telling you what Jeff said. He leaves for U of M next week—freshmen have to go early for orientation. They have a whole week of meetings in the morning and a bunch of social stuff every night. Imagine all the guys you could meet at a place like that!"

Or all the girls, Nikki thought sadly, then replied more sharply than she'd intended, "I thought *Jeremy* was the love of your life!"

Carly looked at her in surprise. "Well, bite my head off, why don't you?"

Nikki was glad she spotted a small stationery store in a tiny strip mall so they could end the conversation right there. Fifteen minutes later, when they had finished buying a "From Both of Us" birthday card and a pin in the shape of a grand piano for Marta, they began looking for the bakery. It turned out to be just a section of the local Piggly Wiggly grocery market, marked off by a long counter and swathed in the warm, yeasty smell of freshly baked bread. Behind the counter, a short, stocky woman in a white smock presided. She reminded Nikki of her grandmother, the way she'd been before her stroke, quick and sure in all her move-ments as she deftly removed sugar cookies from a baking sheet to huge cooling racks spread out across the counter.

"We need a Boston cream pie, please," Nikki said.

"Be right with you, girls. Just let me get these cookies off the hot pan before they overbake." She shoveled the last cookie onto the rack, placed the pan and turner into a huge stainless-steel sink, then looked up and smiled. "Okay. Now what can I do for you?"

"We need a Boston cream pie," they both said together, then looked at each other and laughed.

"Oh, great," Carly said, sounding more like her old self than she had in several days, "now we're into synchronized talking!"

"Well," the counter lady replied, "no matter how you ask, I'm afraid I can't help you. We only make a few of them each week, and I sold the last one about a half hour ago. We have a real nice chocolate cherry layer cake here." She pointed to a chocolate-frosted double layer cake decorated with cherries.

Nikki's mouth watered at the sight of the dark frosting, but she shook her head. "It's for my aunt's birthday, and she doesn't like cherries. Boston cream is her favorite. Thanks, anyway." She turned to Carly as they walked out of the Piggly Wiggly together. "Great. Now what do we do? I'm sure that's the only bakery in a town this small."

"Well," Carly said as they climbed back into the white Taurus and pulled the doors shut behind them, "at least we got the present and a card." She reached around and picked up a magazine from the seat behind them, then searched through the pages. "Okay, Nik. Today's quiz is the one about lips. 'Lipliner, Lipstick, Gloss, or Pencil—Which One's Best for You?' We were going to do that one yesterday, but we didn't have time."

"I didn't know you brought that thing along," Nikki said.

"Had to. We'll never find time to do these quizzes back at the house," Carly answered. "And this is like the most important thing I want to get done on this whole trip."

"You must be really gone on this Jeremy guy. I hope he's worth it."

Carly stared out the window with a happy smile and a faraway look in her eyes. "No problem there, Nik. No problem at all!"

When they pulled into the driveway back at the house, Tory and Marissa were just coming out of the barn, each with a kitten in her arms.

"Carly! Hey, Carly!" Tory called, running toward them. "Want to see my kitten now?"

And hello to you, too, Tory, Nikki said to herself. *Thanks for letting me know I'm all but invisible.* She put the Taurus in park and pulled the key out of the ignition, ashamed of her jealousy. *There could be worse things, sure. But then, that's the way it's always been when I'm with Carly. Next to her, I just fade away.*

Carly oohed and aahed over Tory's calico kitten, cuddling it in her hands, stroking the orange, black, and white fur with one careful finger.

"She's so tiny!" she exclaimed, holding the fragile creature against her cheek, nuzzling it.

There was a faint "mew" from the kitten's pink mouth, then the sound of purring as the animal settled down in Carly's hands.

"Where'd you two go?" Marissa asked, struggling to keep her own black and white kitten, which seemed hyperactive compared to Tory's, from jumping to the ground.

"To the store—Piggly Wiggly," Nikki answered. "It's my aunt's birthday today, and we were trying to get her a

Boston cream pie, but they were all out, so we ended up with just a present and a card."

"Couldn't you get her some other kind of cake?" Marissa asked.

"Aunt Marta doesn't really like sweets much. She just has this thing about Boston cream pie, but I guess she'll have to do without this time."

"Why don't we make one for her?" Marissa asked, and Nikki was struck by the kindness in her eyes.

"Here?"

"Sure. Dr. Phyllis lets us do stuff in her kitchen all the time. She really loves to cook, but she says it's not so much fun alone. She taught us to make pita bread a couple weeks ago. You want to try one of these Boston cream pies?"

Nikki hesitated, then realized Marissa was offering a lot more than a chance to cook together. She smiled and said, "Sure," but her answer was drowned out by Marissa's sudden yelp of pain. The black and white kitten, annoyed at being restrained so long, had sunk its razor-sharp teeth into the tender, fleshy part of the girl's hand at the base of her right thumb.

The kitten dropped to the driveway in a flash of black fur and dashed for the barn. Marissa grabbed her hand and squeezed it hard, dancing around with pain.

"Ouch!" Nikki commiserated. "That must really hurt. Come on inside, and we'll wash it off and get some medicine on it." She circled Marissa's shoulders with her arm, glanced back at Carly and Tory as they ran after the black kitten, and turned toward the house.

❧ *Seven* ❧

BY THE TIME NIKKI HAD WASHED Marissa's hand, smeared antibiotic ointment over the small, bleeding punctures, and applied a bandage, Carly and Tory were back from corralling both kittens in the barn.

"I've *always* wanted to jog!" Tory was saying as she slammed the screen door behind them.

"That's good, Tory," Carly answered. "Maybe you can go with me some morning. It really helps to keep your weight down."

Nikki looked at Tory's thin middle beneath the yellow crop top and raised an eyebrow in question. Carly didn't notice, however, and the kittens and Marissa's injured hand were all immediately forgotten once Tory heard the plans to make a Boston cream pie.

"I love to bake!" Tory said, springing into action. She dragged a stool in front of the refrigerator and teetered back and forth on it to reach the cupboards overhead and rummage through the cookbooks stacked there.

Nikki held her breath as Tory wobbled and grabbed at the top edge of the refrigerator door to steady herself.

"Tory, you better get down before you break your neck!" Nikki said.

Carly dismissed her concern with a casual wave of her hand. "Nikki, you always get so uptight about everything." She crossed to where Tory stood and braced her hands against the stool. "All she needs is a little help. Go on, Tory, get what you want."

Tory dragged a thick volume titled *Grand Finales* off the shelf. "This is Dr. Phyllis's favorite cookbook for desserts. I'll bet Boston cream pie is in here."

It seemed no time at all till the wide white counter was covered with dirty bowls and flour. Nikki, still simmering over Carly's comment, watched Tory beat the cake mixture with a wire whip, sending a spray of the gooey, golden batter spattering onto the white floor. Marissa, who was melting chocolate and butter together in a large glass measuring cup in the microwave, rolled her eyes.

"Tory, look at the mess you're making!" She nodded toward the floor and added, "Dr. Phyllis will skin you alive if you don't get that all cleaned up."

The only sign that Tory had heard was that she whisked the batter faster and snapped her ever-present bubble gum even more loudly than usual. She went on listening to Carly, who ran her finger around the edge of the mixing bowl and popped the batter into her mouth.

Marissa watched, wide-eyed. "My mother says you shouldn't do that because of the raw eggs. You could get food poisoning!"

Carly and Tory glanced at each other and burst out laughing.

"Really. You could!" Marissa insisted.

"Don't worry," Carly said with mock seriousness, "I won't eat any more, Marissa." She scooped out another fingerful of batter and held it up. "I'll just rub it right on my hips, since that's where it'll all end up anyhow!"

"Oooh, gross!" Tory laughed even harder as Marissa's cheeks flushed bright red, then the younger girl turned back to Carly. "Anyway, you'd never have to worry about *your* hips, Carly. Or anything else," she added, eyeing her new idol's figure enviously.

"Oh, right! That's what you think! You wouldn't believe how hard it is to keep up with an exercise routine when you're traveling. I got this terrific hour-long exercise video back in Chicago, and I was doing aerobics with it every single day till we started this trip."

"An hour every day?" Tory asked. "You both exercise an hour *every day?*"

"No, we both don't. *I* do. Nik's not into self-improvement. Or anything else that means change."

Nikki tried to protest, but Carly went on, looking down at her own middle.

"I haven't even been able to weigh myself since we got here. I've looked all over and there's not a single scale in this whole place. Can you believe it?"

"We have a scale at our house," Tory answered. "You could come over and weigh yourself there and see where I live and see the box I've got fixed up for the kittens and—"

But Carly was looking at Tory's freckled face with new interest. "Could I? Come over and use the scale, I mean? I really do need to make sure I haven't gained any weight."

"Oh, come off it, Carly," Nikki said. "How can you act so concerned about gaining weight when you have—" She was about to say "all that junk food stashed under your bed" but suddenly realized that she'd give away her snooping if she did. She backtracked and said, "I mean, how can someone with such a great figure be concerned about gaining weight?"

Carly laughed off her comment with a shrug. "Right,

Nik. You always did know how to rub things in, didn't you?"

Nikki frowned and started to defend herself, but the microwave timer began to beep and she went to help Marissa, who was struggling to get the measuring cups from a cupboard too high for her.

"By the way, Nik," Carly said, "what'd your aunt think of that tape you and Callan made last night of that girl singing?"

Nikki shrugged, not in any frame of mind to answer Carly kindly. "She said she'd listen to it this morning."

"Who'd you tape?" Tory asked. "Was there someone really good at the festival?"

Carly nodded. "Yeah, some skinny little kid with freckles. Annie somebody. She was actually a pretty good singer."

"She was terrific, Carly, admit it," Nikki put in, but her words were lost beneath Tory's.

"You mean Annie Slayton?"

Nikki nodded. "Uh-huh. Callan said she's good friends with you, Marissa."

"She's Marissa's *best* friend. They're always riding horses together and going off on walks and stuff so they can talk. *Privately.*" Tory's expression said clearly what she thought about people who went off on "walks and stuff" and left her behind.

Marissa stirred the chocolate and butter mixture together. "It's the only way we can ever get a word in edgewise, Tory. It's not like we can talk with *you* around." She licked the chocolate off the spoon. "Besides, we have to make the most of every minute. We don't get to see each other much, her dad being the way he is."

"What do you mean, 'the way he is'?" Nikki asked.

Marissa shrugged. "Well, he's just kind of . . . kind of . . ."

She hesitated, searching for the right word, but Tory, as usual, had no such problem.

"Drunk," the younger girl finished flatly. "Most of the time. And there's nothing 'kind of' about it."

Carly and Nikki both looked at Marissa for confirmation, and she nodded.

"I just didn't want to say it straight out like that. Annie always tries to cover for him. She gets really embarrassed if people find out."

Carly gave a short "huff" as she scraped the last drops of golden batter into the cake tin and slid it into the oven. "If he's drunk all the time, how can people help but find out?"

"He's not around people much," Marissa answered. "He works in the woods. He used to have some other job, but he's a lumberjack now. He cuts up on Back Mountain mostly, then skids the logs out and trucks come and take them to the mill down in Lima. Sometimes Annie's the only one who sees him for a couple weeks at a time."

"And wishes she didn't," Tory put in.

"Hush up, Tory!" her older sister said, cracking her knuckles anxiously. "You're always blabbing things, you know that? That's why we don't talk in front of you."

"Well, it's true, isn't it?" Tory said. "You know as well as I do that he's as mean as a snake to Annie. Else why does she come running to our house bawling all the time? Huh? And stop cracking your knuckles."

"Stop popping your gum!" Marissa shot back.

Nikki's glance met Carly's, and the old sense of working together was back in place again, at least for a moment.

Nikki took Dr. Phyllis's apron off its hook and tied it around her middle.

"Cleanup time. You guys bring all the bowls and stuff over here, and I'll load them in the dishwasher."

"Right," Carly seconded her. "We've gotta get this kitchen back the way it was. We don't want Marta to know what we've been doing or it'll ruin the surprise."

Tory looked back and forth from one to another. "Yeah, sure. You're just trying to shut me up. I know."

Tory's and Carly's cleanup efforts didn't last long, however. As they worked, Carly started telling Tory about the 30-day makeover magazine, and within minutes, Tory decided she'd like to see it. The next thing Nikki knew, they were on their way out the door, headed to where the car was parked.

She called after them, sputtering, but Marissa stopped her.

"It's no use, Nikki," she said.

"What do you mean?" Nikki asked, rinsing the last of the melted chocolate out of the glass measuring cup.

"Tory only hears what she wants to, especially when it comes to work."

"Sounds like someone else I know," Nikki said. The two girls looked at each other, then burst out laughing together. "Well, we got most of it done, anyway. It won't take long to finish up here."

They worked side by side quietly for a minute till Callan came into the kitchen for a can of soda. He took a long drink, then rolled his eyes as he surveyed the mess.

"Sure glad I never learned to do dishes. I think I'll get out of here while I can."

"Thanks a lot!" Nikki called, laughing at the face Marissa made toward Callan's retreating back.

After the click of his crutches died away down the hall, Nikki asked a question she'd been wondering about. "Marissa, why's Callan on crutches? I mean, I know he has a problem with his leg, but what caused it?"

Marissa looked up from the dishwasher in surprise.

"You didn't know? He has muscular dystrophy."

"Oh." Nikki worked for another minute, spraying out the sink, then stopped. "But muscular dystrophy keeps getting worse and worse, doesn't it?"

"That's what my father says," the younger girl answered, her voice quiet.

Marissa picked up the wet dishcloth and began scrubbing at droplets of cake batter that had dried on the white counter before she spoke. When she did, she tried to make her voice sound nonchalant.

"So you really thought Annie was good, huh?"

By noon, when the last bit of batter was off the counter and floor, and the dishwasher dry cycle finally clicked off, Tory and Carly wandered back into the kitchen. Nikki was putting the finishing touches on their creation.

"So what are we gonna do now?" Tory asked, watching Nikki set the finished Boston cream pie, filled with vanilla pudding and glazed with chocolate, on a shelf in the refrigerator.

"Lay out in the sun, I hope," Nikki answered. "I'm beat."

"Are you kidding?" Carly asked. "You're the one who was teasing me about being an old lady, but you're aging fast, girl! Now that the cake's all done, I think we ought to take Tory and Marissa up on their offer and visit their house."

Visit their house, sure, but I didn't think we'd be imitating mountain goats to get there, Nikki was thinking 10 minutes later as she grasped the branch of a young sassafras tree and struggled to keep her footing on a section of footpath that was as steep as anything she'd ever walked on before. They were on the "shortcut," as Tory called it, over the hill behind Dr. Brummels's house.

Even Marissa was short of breath as she warned Nikki, "Be sure and watch where you're going. The groundhogs make big holes up here that are really dangerous even for the horses. They could break a leg if they stepped in one."

Tory was already near the crest of the hill, waiting impatiently. "I knew you'd rather come this way. It's a lot shorter."

"Of course, she neglected to mention that it's straight up," Nikki muttered.

"Oh, quit being such a grouch," Carly shot back. "You've got to understand she's just a kid, Nik."

Well, thank you, Miss Goodness and Light, Nikki thought, irritated. *When exactly did you become such an expert on understanding kids?*

But she kept her question to herself, partly because Carly was so short-tempered these days, and partly because once they'd passed the crest of the hill and started down the other side, Carly talked both Tory and Marissa into jogging the rest of the way. And, of course, Nikki had to follow.

✾ *Eight* ✾

TORY AND MARISSA'S FAMILY lived in a single-story brown house with once-white window trim that had yellowed and flaked in the hot Virginia sunshine. A red panel truck was parked in the gravel drive beside the house. On the side of the truck, the words Holsom Bread were painted beneath a six-foot loaf of bread with golden-crusted white slices spilling artistically from an open bread bag.

Overgrown honeysuckle ranged along the side of the large front porch, and from the cool, dirt-floored crawl space underneath the bushes emerged a hound. It barked a deep, throaty sound, then sat down suddenly and scratched gingerly with its hind paw at one large drooping ear.

"Hey, McGee!" Tory dropped to her knees in the dirt beside the hound, then turned her head to explain over her shoulder. "This is Daddy's best hunting dog." She stopped to inspect McGee's ear carefully. "You got another tick, boy?"

"Yuck," Marissa said. "Ticks are the grossest things in the world. You better let Daddy take care of it, Tory."

"Don't be such a chicken, Marissa. I know how to get

ticks out just as well as he does. He showed me. You would, too, if you weren't so prissy about everything."

Another hound emerged from under the porch, and Carly turned and moved away as though walking out a leg cramp. But Nikki saw the laughter in her eyes before she turned and went after her.

"What's so funny?" Nikki asked in a low voice when she reached Carly's side.

Carly's laugh was muffled, and she shook her head. "Can you believe it, Nik? This place is like redneck heaven. I mean, look at the house. And hounds under the porch." In a drawn-out, exaggerated drawl, she added, "Pure Southern redneck."

Nikki started to laugh, too, but when Carly rolled her eyes mockingly, her laughter stopped. Suddenly, she saw Carly's humor in a different light. It seemed as if Carly were compelled to tear other people down these days. First, there was the way she treated Callan, and now this.

It's almost like she makes herself feel more important when she treats other people this way.

The wooden front door opened, and a woman with Tory's brown eyes and Marissa's tentative smile stepped out onto the porch.

"Tory," she said, wiping her hands on a red plaid dish-towel, "leave the ticks to your father, please." Then her glance swept the rest of the yard and stopped at Carly and Nikki.

Tory was quick with introductions. "This is Carly Allen, Mama. And Nikki," she added, as though she'd just remembered there were two of them standing there. "Nikki—" she hesitated, then turned to face her. "What was your last name again, Nik? I can't remember."

"Sheridan," Marissa whispered sharply, but Tory was

already off on her description of why Carly and Nikki were at Dr. Brummels's house.

"So glad to meet both of you," their mother said, rubbing her hands more vigorously on the towel, then extending her right hand to each of them to shake. "My name is Lou. Lou Barker. Won't you come in and meet my husband?"

Nikki glanced at Carly as if to say, *Nothing redneck about her manners, is there?* But Carly was already moving toward the front door.

They stepped into a small hallway, and Nikki could see a small front room furnished modestly with a blue-flowered, slip-covered couch and two recliners. Then they turned the opposite direction into an equally small kitchen. A large man sat at the table with his back to them, working hard over a plate heaped with spaghetti. Red hairs bristled down the back of his thick, tanned neck.

"Yarnell," Lou called, but there was no response. "Yarnell!" she said louder as she crossed to the sink and hung up the dishtowel on a towel rack.

Nikki winced. The man didn't even have the manners to respond. The hunting hounds, the whole backwoods setting, the way he ignored them all—Nikki hated to admit it, but maybe Carly's assessment was right after all.

Then Marissa went to her father's side and laid her hand on his shoulder. He started and turned to face her, then saw the others. As he did, Nikki could see the hearing aid in his right ear, and her thoughts did a U-turn.

Mr. Barker pushed back his chair with a scraping sound on the green-and-brown linoleum and got to his feet hurriedly, towering over all of them with a wide smile.

"Pardon me. Didn't even hear you come in." He gestured at the hearing aid, and Nikki noted there was barely a tinge of Southern drawl in his words.

"We're just going to show Nikki—this is Nikki," Marissa interrupted herself, pointing in Nikki's direction, "and that's Carly, and they're staying at Dr. Phyllis's house for a couple weeks while Nikki's aunt works on a book. Anyway, we're just going to show them around."

"And Daddy?" Tory said. The big man put an arm around her and tilted his head in her direction. "McGee's got another tick. I can tell from the way he's pawing at his ear."

Yarnell Barker nodded, reassuring her. "I'll take care of it right after I eat. Don't you worry, honey. Won't you all have some lunch with me? The delivery route brought me close by the house today, so Lou fixed spaghetti for me." He looked at his daughters. "And you know your mother—there's plenty for everyone."

Marissa and Tory moved toward the table without hesitation, and Yarnell hurried to bring two folding chairs from an enclosed porch off the kitchen. Nikki sat down, sniffing the scent of herbs and tomato sauce, and realized that even though there had been a lot of licking spoons and tasting batter when they baked at Dr. Brummels's earlier that day, they'd never actually gotten around to lunch.

Carly will love this, she thought. *She can never resist spaghetti.*

Carly sat with them but held up both hands when Lou passed around the serving bowl heaped with pasta.

"Thank you very much," she said, "but if you don't mind, I'll just have some of the iced tea."

"You must be sick," Nikki joked. She looked around the table at the others. "I've known her for 15 years, and I've *never* seen her turn down spaghetti."

"I'm not sick," Carly replied deliberately, and once again there was that surprising edge of sharpness to her words. "I'm just being careful."

Across the table from Nikki, Tory looked up from the serving spoons laden with spaghetti that she held suspended over her plate. She glanced at the sauce-covered pasta and swallowed hard, then dropped it back into the serving bowl.

"Me, too. I have to be careful, too."

Lou Barker gave a comfortable laugh. "Good grief, Tory, what have you got to be careful about? Since day one, you've never had an extra ounce of fat anywhere on your body!"

But Tory drew herself up to her full height with dignity. "I'll just have tea, too. Please."

"Well, now, I don't know as I can go along with that," Tory's father said. He darted a glance at Carly, obviously not wanting to make her uncomfortable, but struggling with concern for his daughter.

"Daddy—" Tory began.

"No, listen to me, honey. It's one thing to be a young lady like Carly and Nikki here. But you're only 11, and your body's growing. You need to eat."

"So now I'm a *baby*?" Tory protested. "I can't even make up my mind about whether or not I'm hungry just because I'm 11?"

"Tell you what," Carly said, stepping in. "How about we have just a little, Tory? Will it be okay if she just eats a small plateful, Mr. Barker?"

Carly's decision seemed to settle the matter, but Nikki couldn't help but notice how uncomfortable Carly looked as she ate.

After lunch, Yarnell Barker removed the tick from McGee's floppy ear and then, with a quick kiss to each of his girls, pulled away in the Holsom Bread truck. Carly and Nikki followed Tory and Marissa down the hall to the bedroom they shared. Nikki was amused to see a thick line of light-brown masking tape marking the middle of the green carpet.

On the left side of the tape, a pink-striped comforter was pulled up haphazardly over a twin bed, lumpy with bulges that gave away the rumpled sheets underneath. A white nightshirt adorned with a picture of Garfield lay in a heap on the floor, and beside it was an open package of red licorice Twizzlers. Posters and pictures crowded the wall beside the bed, every inch of white plaster covered.

On the right side of the masking tape, an identical pink-striped comforter covered another twin bed with hardly a wrinkle. Pillows of all sizes, covered with lace shams, were arranged neatly at the head of the bed. Only one picture graced the wall here—a print of a graceful ballerina in midpirouette.

"You'll have to excuse the way the room looks," Marissa said, with a pointed glance in her little sister's direction.

But Tory, on the floor rummaging beneath the lumpy bed, was oblivious to Marissa's words. More and more of her disappeared from sight, till only her thin rump and legs protruded.

Finally, there was a muffled "Got it!" from under the bed, and Tory wriggled out backward until she could stand up again. She held up a sheaf of glossy magazine pages in front of the other girls.

"See?" she said. "I saved this whole section from one of Mama's magazines. It's all about how you should take care of your new kitten and how to train it and stuff. Wanna look at it with me, Carly?"

Carly arranged herself cross-legged on Tory's bed and listened politely, but Nikki could sense her edginess. Nikki watched Carly curiously, knowing she was anxious to do something else.

She's usually so impatient with younger kids—especially Abby and Adam, her own younger sister and brother. Either she really, really likes Tory, or there's something else going on here.

The talk progressed from cats to a discussion about Tory's hair and all the different styles Carly could figure out for her. When they'd tried four or five, Tory finally settled on a French braid. Carly's fingers flew, weaving the long, brown strands of hair together expertly.

"How many dogs does your father have?" she asked as she worked.

"Just two," Tory answered. "He doesn't get much time to hunt, though. He's too busy with his job."

"I can imagine," Carly said smugly, and Nikki knew she was comparing Yarnell Barker and his bread truck with her own father, a successful doctor in Chicago.

But Marissa caught her tone and spoke up. "My dad's busy because he's starting his own business. He's got a degree in computer science, and he's only driving a bread truck till the business starts making money."

Carly glanced at Marissa, surprise flickering in her eyes for an instant, then she carefully finished the braid and fastened a little white bow at the end. Nikki had to admit, the style did flatter Tory. Her brown eyes brightened as she surveyed her reflection in the mirror, and a pink flush of pleasure tinged her high cheekbones.

"This looks so great, Carly. Thank you!" She turned and hugged Carly. "You can do just about anything, can't you? Could you teach me how to put on makeup? Like you do?"

Carly considered this. "Do you have any makeup? Either of you?"

"No, my parents won't let me wear it," Tory answered. "They say I'm too young. And Marissa doesn't use makeup."

"Well, if your parents say it's okay, I'll use some of mine

on you sometime when you come over."

"Oh, good. I'll ask! Come on out to the barn with me now, and I'll show you the box I fixed up for the kittens."

But Nikki could tell Carly had reached the end of her patience.

"I'll tell you what, Tory, Nik and I have to get back soon. So why don't we have a quick look at the barn on our way out?"

"Sure," Tory responded with an *anything you say!* look and moved toward the door.

"But first, remember you said you had a scale here?" Carly asked. "Could you show me where it is?"

"I forgot all about that! Come on, it's in the bathroom," Tory said.

While they were waiting for Carly to come out of the bathroom, the hounds began barking furiously outside the house. There was a knock at the door and then voices, first Lou Barker's gentle tones, then an urgent voice that spilled out painful words. Nikki heard footsteps hurrying down the hall.

"Annie!" Marissa burst out, moving quickly toward her friend. "What's the matter? Did he—?" She stopped in mid-sentence and both of them glanced at Nikki and Tory, then at Carly, who emerged from the bathroom.

Nikki studied Annie's face—the same face she'd watched bent over a guitar at the festival the night before. Only now, the girl's heavy eyeshadow and blush were gone. In their place were pale lips and sandy-brown lashes framing light-brown eyes, rimmed with red that showed she'd been crying. Instead of the skin-tight miniskirt and boots, she now wore faded, frayed jeans shorts topped by a blue and white striped T-shirt. She looked even younger than she had at the festival—and more fragile.

Tory, totally missing the look that passed between

Marissa and Annie, burst out, "Annie, look how Carly did my hair!" She twirled around to show the back. "And she's going to show me how to use makeup, if it's okay with Mom and Dad. I bet she'd show you, too, if you want."

"No, thanks! I have to spend enough time in makeup as it is, ever since Dad got it in his mind to make me into some kind of—" She broke off, then finished in a gentler tone. "Another time, okay, Tory?"

It was easy to see that Marissa and Annie needed to talk. Nikki caught Carly's eye and nodded toward the door.

"We've got to get back," Nikki said. "We didn't even tell Aunt Marta or Dr. Brummels where we were going, and I don't want them to worry. Come on, Carly."

It wasn't till they were out the door and partway up the path toward the crest of the hill that the real trouble started.

❦ *Nine* ❧

"HEY!" CARLY CALLED from somewhere behind Nikki. "You think you could manage to wait up there, Wonderwoman?"

Nikki swung around and was surprised to see Carly suddenly drop her mocking tone and bend over double, hands on her knees.

"What're you doing way back there?" Nikki teased. "Can't keep up, huh?" She crossed her arms over her chest and tapped her foot with exaggerated impatience as she stared at the sky. "Hmmm, don't I remember a certain person telling me just this morning how great all this exercise would be for me? Looks like all that jogging and exercising aren't doing too much for you!"

Carly didn't answer. Instead, she straightened up slowly, her face white and her eyes as wide as if she'd seen a snake in the path. She gulped in several long breaths of air, then the frightened look faded to a scowl.

"Hey! Are you okay?" Nikki asked. "Carly?" She ran back down the path toward her friend. "Maybe you shouldn't be exercising so much and pushing yourself all the time."

Carly seemed to catch her breath then. She started uphill once again. But instead of laughing as she caught up with Nikki, Carly muttered, "What I do about exercising is my own business, so why don't you just leave me alone, okay?"

Startled, Nikki burst out, *"What?"* but found herself talking to Carly's black-shirted back. "Carly!" she yelled after her. "What are you so *steamed* about these days?"

Carly turned, framed between the two loblolly pines that grew on either side of the path. Hazy sunlight filtered down between the branches onto Carly's golden hair, and the thought flitted through Nikki's mind that the picture would make a great magazine cover. But the minute Carly opened her mouth, the illusion was shattered.

"You want to know what I'm so *steamed* about? Fine! I'll *tell* you what I'm steamed about! The only thing you ever do anymore is criticize me. All I'm trying to do is set a few goals for myself, make myself a little better. And what do I get from you? You're supposed to be one of my best friends in the whole, entire world, and you tell me I'm *nuts*. You tell me I can't see *reality*. You think it's easy losing weight, Nikki? Of all people, *you* should know how tough it is! It's only been a couple months since you were pregnant and big as a house, remember? What I need from you is encouragement, not put-downs, okay?"

"But Carly—"

Carly raked both hands through her hair, combing it back off her face. "And another thing. You've changed, Nikki. Big time. We used to tell each other things, remember? Like what was going on in our lives. Well, ever since last summer, you and Jeff started having all your secret conversations—and left me out in the cold. Ever since you got pregnant, you've acted like I'm just not *good* enough for you to talk to anymore!"

"But—"

"Don't you *'but'* me, Nikki Sheridan! Who was it you told first? Huh? It sure wasn't *me*. And who was it you ran to every time something went wrong during the pregnancy? My brother, my parents—anybody but me. I hoped coming along on this trip would make things like they used to be between us, but it's not working at all. You won't even cooperate. And now whatever's going on with you and Jeff is off limits, too."

That's because there is *nothing going on with me and Jeff anymore,* Nikki wanted to yell back in frustration. *And because it hurts too much to talk about it with* anyone, *especially with you.*

But Carly wasn't finished. "And all you ever do these days is tell me what I'm doing wrong. Well, let me tell you, I don't think this is much of a friendship, *if* you don't mind my saying so!" Carly turned on one foot and started up the path again.

Nikki didn't even try to defend herself. All those ideas she'd had about her and Carly having devotions and praying together, about getting back to the way they used to be, popped like so many bubbles in her head before the angry words Carly threw like darts.

And the worst part was that so much of what Carly was saying was true. Nikki *had* changed. *No one could go through what I've been through this past year and not change,* she thought. But all this time, she'd only been thinking about how the situation was affecting her.

Yet now, for just an instant, it was as though she stood in Carly's shoes, seeing the world through *her* eyes.

Nikki shook her head, trying to clear it. Carly, the life of the party, feeling left out? Carly, needing *her*? Talk about a switch. It was as if she'd looked at the sky and it was suddenly green instead of blue. But even Carly's heated confession didn't explain everything she was doing.

"Carly!" she called after the retreating black shirt.

There was no answer.

"Carly, I'm talking to you! Maybe you're right about a lot of the things you said. But that's only part of it. I think there's something else going on here, and we need to talk about it!"

Carly reached the crest of the hill and started down the other side without so much as a glance over her shoulder. Nikki hung her head and trudged up the path behind her.

What'd I do wrong this time? she asked herself. *I sure said something that flipped her switch.* She racked her brains, playing back the conversation.

All I did was tease her about the exercise. Something clicked in her mind then, and it was like watching a playback of the scene at dinner the day before. *That was all Callan did, too— tease her about the guy back in Chicago. And he's been on her blacklist ever since.*

It made no sense. None.

Now, if it were me, *with these extra pounds superglued to my waist since Evan was born, I'd have a legitimate reason to get upset.*

"Not that it'd do me any good," she muttered to herself. "Even if I did lose those last five pounds, I'd still never look like Carly."

She reached up to smooth back her unruly, shoulder-length hair that curled even more wildly than usual in the Virginia humidity. She was so totally unlike Carly, who looked the same every day—perfect.

Anyway, it couldn't be just the exercise thing that was getting Carly all worked up. But there was the thing about Jeff. Nikki had crossed the crest of the hill and held on to the limb of the small sassafras tree once again as she started down the near-vertical section of the path.

Well, at least that's something I can make Carly understand. It'd be hard, sure, because she didn't want to talk about Jeff—it still hurt way too much to know that she'd allowed him to walk right out of her life. *No, be honest, Nikki, you pushed him out of your life.*

But for the sake of getting her friendship with Carly back to the way it used to be, she could do it. Nikki slid a foot or two down the rest of the steep section, then quickened her pace. She'd talk it out with Carly as soon as she could catch up.

But Carly was so far ahead that Nikki didn't catch up till they reached the edge of Dr. Brummels's yard.

"Hey! Carly!" she panted, an apology worked out in her head.

Carly turned with a quick grin and spoke as though the sharp words between them had never happened.

"So who's a slowpoke now? Hmmm? Come on, we've gotta make sure everything's set for your aunt's birthday. I was thinking, why don't we really go all out and put up a bunch of balloons and get that shiny foil confetti for the table. And candles—we have to have lots of candles. We can just stick 'em in the Boston cream pie. What do you think?"

Nikki, confused, started to answer. "I'm not sure, the top's pretty soft and—"

But Carly rolled right on. "How many candles do we need?"

Nikki calculated for a minute. "We need 33. I always have to stop and figure it out. My mother's 43, and Aunt Marta's 10 years younger. Anyway, how exactly do you plan to come up with balloons and confetti, not to mention 33 candles?"

"Easy," Carly said as she pulled the kitchen screen door open. "We'll just drive back into town. What'll it take us— five minutes?"

As they stepped inside the kitchen, Carly dropped her last words to a whisper and nodded in warning toward Marta and Dr. Brummels, who sat at the table with gray-blue earthenware mugs and Marta's small recorder on the table between them. Annie's voice sang from the device, and every few seconds, Dr. Phyllis pushed *pause* so the two of them could rave about tone quality and pitch and timbre.

"She's just a natural, Marta," Dr. Brummels said. "Musicians like that come along once in a blue moon. It's as though they're born already knowing much of what we try for years to cram into other students. And to think she was right under my nose the whole time and I never even knew it."

"I think we need to do everything we can to make sure she gets the training she needs," Marta said.

Dr. Brummels nodded enthusiastically. "You're right, Marta. We do. Because I can tell you for sure, her father never will!"

Carly filled a glass with ice from the refrigerator door. Dr. Brummels twisted in her chair at the sound.

"Hi, ladies. You're back."

"We were wondering what happened to you," Marta put in, a question in her voice.

Nikki walked to the table and sat down beside her aunt. "Tory and Marissa took us over to their place."

"By way of the road?" Dr. Brummels asked.

"Oh, no. Nothing that easy!" Carly said, groaning as she dropped into the chair beside Nikki. "When Nikki says we went *over* to their place, that's exactly what she means. Over the mountain, on a path about a foot wide."

"Not to mention straight up and down, at least part of the way," Nikki added. "I felt like a mountain goat half the time."

"Are you hungry?" Dr. Phyllis asked. "Marta and I were just talking about having something for a late lunch."

"Nothing for me, thanks," Carly said.

"We ate spaghetti at the Barkers'," Nikki explained.

"Actually," Marta said, getting to her feet, "I'm not all that hungry either, Phyllis." She started toward the refrigerator. "I think I'd like just a soda, okay? The tea was lovely, but I'm ready for something cold."

Carly's eyes met Nikki's, and they both thought of the Boston cream pie sitting prominently on the second shelf. Both of their chairs scraped on the wooden floor as they sprang to their feet.

"I'll get you a soda!" Nikki said at the same instant Carly offered, "Let me get it for you."

Marta turned and eyed them both, one eyebrow higher than the other. "Excuse me? When did you two get so helpful?"

"Just earning my keep, ma'am," said Carly, who walked to the refrigerator and called out the soda flavors Marta could choose from. Nikki, meanwhile, pointed and mouthed "cake" to Dr. Phyllis, who immediately understood and turned to Marta.

"Hey, they're young, Marta. Sit back and let them spoil you a little," she said, sounding completely natural.

Marta turned and looked suspiciously at Nikki, who put on her best innocent look and nodded her agreement with Dr. Phyllis.

"You think we fooled her?" Carly asked. She shut the bedroom door behind her and leaned against it, laughing.

"I don't know," Nikki answered. "It's pretty hard to put anything over on my aunt. You know that." She went to the dresser and pulled open a drawer. "Oh, brother. I thought I was so smart to pack light, but now I'm not so sure."

"What're you changing for now? We've got to get into town and get the candles and stuff for tonight."

"Yeah, I know. That's why I want to change. I got all sweaty going to the Barkers'." She went through the clothes in her drawer. "You know what, Carly? I think I definitely should've brought more stuff."

Carly opened one of her dresser drawers, pulled out a pair of jeans shorts, and held them out to Nikki. "Here. Take these."

"Wait a minute. Let me get this straight." Nikki cocked her head to one side. "Those are your favorite shorts. Borrowing your fingernail polish nearly got me into big-time trouble, and now you're loaning me your favorite shorts?"

Carly thrust the shorts at her so Nikki had to grab them. "I'm not *loaning* them to you, I'm *giving* them away, okay?"

Nikki frowned. "But why?"

Carly looked exasperated. "Because they don't fit. They fall off me, all right?"

Nikki's first thought was, *Thanks a lot! They're too big for you, so they'll fit me?* But Carly had also decided to change, and as she tugged off her shorts and stood in her high-cut bikini underwear, Nikki realized suddenly how sharply her friend's hip bones protruded. Her irritation faded to concern.

"Carly! How much weight have you lost?"

Carly just shook her head and went on changing.

"That's why you've been wearing those huge T-shirts, isn't it?" Nikki demanded. "To hide how much weight you've lost, right?"

"Lay off, Nikki. You sound just like somebody's mother." Carly buttoned a smaller pair of shorts at the waist, but even so, the waistband hung slack around her middle.

Nikki watched her, and suddenly a few more pieces of the puzzle Carly had become began to fit together. *I've got to figure out how to get through to her.*

"Carly, look at me," Nikki ordered.

Carly looked up defiantly. "What?"

"What was wrong back there on the path when we first left the Barkers'?"

A look of irritation crossed Carly's face, and she turned back to the dresser drawer, rummaging through her T-shirts. "I don't have a clue what you're talking about."

"Carly, stop pretending!" Nikki answered. She dropped the jeans shorts on her bed and walked to Carly's side.

Carly had looked up at the sharp tone of her friend's voice, and now they stared at each other in the mirror.

"Something was wrong—wrong enough that you almost asked me for help. You were bent over double, and when you finally stood up, your face was as white as a sheet. What was it, Carly? Tell me!"

Carly's face was red.

Nikki hurried on, before she lost her courage. "It's got something to do with all this weight you've lost, doesn't it? And with the junk food you have stashed under the bed. *Doesn't it?*"

Carly's eyes opened wide, and Nikki knew she'd scored a hit. Carly threw the yellow T-shirt she held back into the drawer and did what she always did when cornered—went on the offensive. She put her hands on her hips and her chin jutted two inches higher in the air.

"You snoop! You rotten snoop." She stopped and threw up her hands in frustration. "This is just what I need—a 'friend' who sticks her nose in every private corner of my life, trying to psychoanalyze me! You don't have any idea what's going on with me, so just butt out, would you?"

"But Carly," Nikki tried again, "something's wrong here. You may be right. I might not have any idea. But I . . . I want to help."

"There's nothing to help, Nikki! Don't you understand? There's nothing wrong here! Besides, even if I had a problem, I would still take care of myself. I may not be a great brain like you, Nikki, but I know how to take care of myself, thank you very much."

Nikki stared back into Carly's furious brown eyes and part of her wondered what on earth she was supposed to do now. The other part was amazed—as always—at how Carly could make being smart sound like a disease.

Then Carly made a little noise like a gasp and her face went totally white again. She held on to the edge of the drawer for a moment, then seemed to regain her balance and dropped down onto the edge of the bed.

"Carly, what's wrong?" Nikki stooped in front of her. "Do you want me to call Aunt Marta? Dr. Phyllis? 911?"

Carly looked at her coldly. "What I want is for you to go away and leave me alone."

Ten

ON SUNDAY, NIKKI WOKE to the sound of a mockingbird running through its morning repertoire in the mimosa tree outside the bedroom window. She stretched luxuriously with her eyes still closed, toes reaching for the end of the mattress, arms extended till her fingertips bumped the wall behind her head.

She smiled, remembering how last night had turned out. It had looked like a sure disaster at first. Carly had been so angry after their conversation that Nikki drove into town alone for candles and confetti, leaving Carly sulking in their bedroom. But after she'd sat through Aunt Marta's party and had a few hours to cool off, Carly had come upstairs sheepishly, apology written all over her face.

Carly said everything Nikki could have hoped for—that she was awfully sorry for losing her temper and that, yes, she *was* losing weight too fast and she knew it. She also admitted she'd felt a little weak on the path home from the Barkers' because her heart was beating "funny," like it had when they'd argued, but it would be okay because she was going to quit all this nonsense.

"I'll start eating right, Nik, I promise. No more skipping meals and then hiding junk food under the bed." She'd looked down at her sneaker-clad feet and added, "And I'll quit exercising so much. I will, really. I've just been acting crazy, Nik, and I'm sorry. It's just that I wanted Jeremy to like me *so much*. You don't know how much."

Nikki had hugged her, thinking about Jeff. *Oh, I know, Carly. I know!*

The mockingbird started up again, and Nikki realized she had to start getting ready for church.

"Hey, Carly?" she asked, stifling a yawn. "You mind if I wear your yellow dress to church this morning?"

There was no answer.

Nikki rolled over to face Carly's bed and opened her eyes. The other bed was empty.

"Carly?" she asked again, knowing already that the room was empty, too. Nikki slid out of bed and crossed the room. She opened the door and looked across the hall at the bathroom. Empty.

The closet door was ajar, and Nikki pulled it all the way open. On the inside doorknob hung Carly's pink nightshirt, printed across the front in black letters, "I'm Tired, I'm Grouchy, Leave Me Alone!" Her running shoes, complete with the blue and white Chicago Cubs laces she always used, were gone.

Nikki's lips tightened. *You promised, Carly Allen! You promised, and you broke your promise.* She slammed the closet door shut, but a calm voice inside her head insisted that she settle down. It lectured her about her overactive imagination. Why, Carly could be downstairs having breakfast, it insisted. She could be . . .

She could be what? Nikki interrupted the voice. *Her running shoes are gone, and that means she's out running again. And something's wrong enough with her heart that she could be in danger.*

She remembered the pale tinge of Carly's skin on the trail the day before and what she'd said about her heart beating "funny," and quickly pulled on her clothes. As she ran barefoot down the stairs, sneakers in hand in case she had to go searching outside, the house seemed bigger than ever, hollow in its early morning silence. Bright sun streamed through the beveled glass of the front door into the entryway, shining an elongated rectangle of light on the polished wood floor.

Nikki darted down the hall to check the kitchen first, but the room stood silent and empty, dim and shadowy as it would be till the sun reached higher in the sky. *Now what do I do?* she wondered. She couldn't wake everyone simply because she was worried.

And if I told anybody what she said about her heart—She knew what Carly would do then, and she didn't want to think about it.

Nikki made her way back out the hall to the entryway. The sunlight seemed to beckon, and she wanted suddenly to be outside, drinking in the bright, unspoiled morning air. She turned the door handle cautiously, careful not to make any noise, and stepped outside onto the front porch.

The mockingbird carried on loudly, trilling first a robin's song, then a sparrow's, and a few crickets still chirped half-heartedly from beneath the dew-covered rhododendrons that surrounded the base of the porch. Nikki listened carefully, trying to decide what was different, then realized that for the first time since they'd arrived in Virginia, the high-pitched sound of the cicadas was stilled until the sun heated the air and drew out their strange buzzing noises.

"Good morning." The quiet voice spoke from behind her, and Nikki jumped, then whirled around to find herself facing Phyllis Brummels. Dr. Brummels sat curled up in the high-backed wicker rocker, tanned hands cupping one of the gray-blue earthenware mugs from which steam curled upward in thin, lazy tendrils.

Her hair was pulled back casually in a loose bun, and a few dark strands that had escaped the hairpins curled gently against the tanned skin of her neck. Dr. Phyllis rearranged the ends of her white cotton robe over her lap and smiled up at Nikki.

"Did I startle you? I'm sorry."

Nikki shrugged. "It's not your fault. I just wasn't expecting anyone else to even be up yet and . . . "

"Really? It looked like you were expecting someone."

Nikki looked at the older woman more closely. "How could you tell?"

"By the worry all over your face," she said. "And because I saw Carly take off jogging down the driveway about 20 minutes ago. Again."

"She did?" Nikki asked, and her heart sank. *There's no way I can catch up with her then.*

Phyllis nodded. "Um-hmm. I sit out here most every morning, so I saw her yesterday, too." She nodded toward the empty wicker rocker beside her. "Why don't you sit with me for a while, Nikki? We haven't had much time to get to know one another yet."

Nikki hesitated. "Well, I have to shower and all that before church."

Phyllis checked her watch. "Church is two hours from now. Does it take you that long?"

Nikki settled herself uneasily beside Dr. Phyllis, wondering what on earth she could think of to talk about. She said the first thing that popped into her head.

"Did you say you sit here every morning?"

"Just about," Dr. Phyllis said. "I especially wanted to

soak up the sunshine this morning. The weatherman says that hurricane down near Florida is supposed to start moving up the coast, and he's predicting some pretty rough storms in a few days, even this far inland. Anyway, no matter what the weather, this is where I do my best thinking. And praying."

Nikki glanced sideways at her, but Dr. Phyllis was relaxed, her hands cradling her mug, her eyes shut.

The professor's voice broke in on her thoughts.

"Do you pray, Nikki?"

No wonder Aunt Marta likes her, Nikki thought. It was hard to decide which woman was more direct, but it seemed safe to bet that neither one had any problem getting right to the point.

"Yeah, some. I mean, I'm learning. I thought it would all just happen automatically once I became a Christian, but . . . but it isn't exactly that way." Nikki stumbled through her answer. "I mean, since Evan was born—" She turned in sudden embarrassment, realizing that Dr. Phyllis might know nothing about what had happened to her the year before and that now she'd have to explain the whole situation.

But Dr. Phyllis smiled a gentle smile in her direction. "Marta told me about your baby."

"Oh." Nikki blew out a long sigh, not sure whether she was relieved or not.

"I think you've been through a great deal for a girl of . . . what? Eighteen?"

Nikki rested one bare foot on her knee and studied her peeling burgundy toenail polish. "Just 17, at least for another three weeks. I guess you're right about me having been through a lot. And some of it was *awful*. But in a way I'm glad now that it all happened. I don't think I would have ever paid much attention to God if I hadn't gotten in such a mess."

Phyllis stopped the rocker and tipped her head to one side, regarding Nikki with serious eyes. "That's a very wise thing to say."

"It is?" Nikki asked, surprised at the warmth in her voice.

Phyllis pushed against the porch floorboards with the toes of one foot and started the rocker moving again. "Sure it is, Nikki. Some people go all their lives and never understand that pain can be a gift."

Nikki frowned. "What do you mean, 'Pain can be a gift'?"

Phyllis rocked for a minute before she replied, and the silence between them filled with the liquid notes of the mockingbird. "I used to wonder, when I was your age, why everybody seemed to end up with some kind of pain in their lives. For some people, like Callan, it's pain from the word *go*. Others, well, they go for years with everything looking just fine, and then things suddenly fall apart on them. Sooner or later, everyone seems to get handed some kind of burden that looks just too big to carry."

That's the way I felt when I got pregnant with Evan. That's the way I still feel, some days. It's like there'll always be a part of me missing, even though I know he's in a great family and all, Nikki wanted to say, but she stopped just in time. She didn't know Dr. Brummels well enough to get into all of that with her.

The older woman went on. "Some people turn away from God when pain comes. They blame Him for sending it, and they fill up with bitterness and resentment. The pain twists them inside. They seem to become more determined than ever to do life their own way.

"But other people—and I have the feeling you're one of them, Nikki—they turn *toward* God. Somehow He gives them enough courage to believe that there's nothing in this world He can't turn to good.

"Pain shows us how we're fooling ourselves, because it snatches all our props right out from under us—all those things that make us think we're in control. Most of us have to meet a situation that's too big for us to handle before we'll take our hands off the driver's wheel and say, 'Here, God. I can't do this. *You* be in charge from now on.' That's why I say pain is a gift."

Dr. Phyllis's voice had grown quiet, and her eyes were fixed on the horizon. Nikki sat perfectly still, sensing there was some deeply personal memory replaying itself in Dr. Phyllis's mind. Then, with a little shake of her head, she seemed to remember where she was and turned to Nikki.

"The question is, what's God trying to do through the pain Carly's in right now?"

It was Nikki's turn to shake her head then, trying to clear it. She felt as if they'd just taken a quantum leap into unmapped territory. Then the older woman's glance met and held hers, and she was surprised that she hadn't seen it before. It all fit—Carly's sudden outbursts of anger, the way she was putting people down, what she was doing to her body. Something had to be hurting her down deep inside.

After a few minutes, Nikki spoke, slowly. "Maybe you're right—about Carly being in pain, I mean. But how do you know God's trying to do something through it?"

Dr. Phyllis gave a little laugh. "Oh, Nikki, you can absolutely depend on it that God is always trying to reach us when He lets us go through pain. See, sometimes we get the idea God is passive and silent. We think we have to pursue Him. But once we start getting to know Him, we find out that it was *Him* who was pursuing *us* all the time. He allows us to have that gift of pain to get our attention, just like you said happened to you."

Nikki frowned. Christianity had sounded so simple when Jeff explained it to her the year before. You were a sinner. Christ took your punishment on the cross. You believed and—*viola!*—you were on your way to heaven. But it occurred to Nikki suddenly that there might be more to being a Christian than just having her sins forgiven and getting to heaven someday. A whole lot more.

"You're frowning, Nikki. What's the matter?"

"Well," she began, not sure how to go on, "I . . . I'm starting to wish I'd read the fine print. About being a Christian, you know?"

Dr. Phyllis put back her head and laughed loud and long. Finally, she wiped her eyes and shook her head. "Oh, I *do* know. I do!" Then her voice turned serious. "But even if you had read the 'fine print' as you say, you'll never regret becoming a Christian. It just may be different from what you expected. And you'll want to ask *why?* But that's the wrong question. It's not *why*—it's *who?*"

Nikki frowned in concentration. "I'm sorry, Dr. Phyllis. Maybe I'm kind of dense, but that last thing you said—I don't get it."

Dr. Phyllis smiled again. "You're not dense at all, my dear. I've been working at understanding the Christian faith for more years than you've been alive, and I still have to work at it frequently. All I know is, God doesn't usually give me explanations. He just gives me Himself. It may not make sense to you now, but it will. In the future. Anyway, back to your friend Carly. It's obvious that there's something going on with her."

The screen door creaked, and they both swung around to face Marta. She returned their greetings and crossed to the wicker settee that faced their rockers and sat down.

"We were just discussing what's going on with Carly," Dr. Phyllis explained.

"I know," Marta said. "I heard the last bit." She arranged her robe around her legs and took a sip of coffee from her mug. "We were hoping this trip would get her mind off things—change her focus and help her snap out of it. But it doesn't seem to be working."

Nikki sat up straight and brought the rocker to a halt. "*We?* We who? I thought Carly just came along on this trip for fun."

Marta's forehead creased into the two vertical lines that always showed between her eyebrows when she got upset. "Well, she did. Partly."

Nikki waited, staring at her aunt. When she didn't go on, Nikki urged her, "What do you mean, 'partly'?"

Marta drew her legs up under her on the settee. "As far as Carly and you are supposed to know, this was to be just a vacation. A time for you two to be together and have fun. The Allens thought being around you would be good for her."

Nikki's head was swimming at this sudden climb in the Allens's estimation of her. All year long, she'd been the problem child, and now they thought *she* might be good for *Carly?* That was a switch.

Nikki decided to keep the conversation focused. "And as far as we're *not* supposed to know?" she asked.

"Carly's parents were getting worried. They came to me a few weeks before this trip and said they felt she needed a break."

Nikki's frustration boiled over. "Aunt Marta, we're just going around in circles here! Would you please stop avoiding my questions?"

"Finessing," Dr. Phyllis murmured.

Nikki looked at her, irritated. "What?"

"Finessing. It sounds so much better than *avoiding*, don't you think?" Dr. Phyllis waggled her eyebrows, and Nikki burst out laughing.

"I'm sorry. I didn't mean to be rude, Aunt Marta. Just

please, tell me what's going on with Carly."

"Why don't you tell me what you think's going on, Nik?" Marta countered. "I'd be interested in hearing your opinion first."

Nikki swallowed her impatience and concentrated on putting into words what she was stretching to understand.

"She's not like she used to be. At least, not most of the time. I mean, she used to be so fun and laid-back, always making everybody laugh and stuff. But now—one minute she bites my head off because I borrow her nail polish, and the next minute she's smiling at me like everything's normal. Then two minutes later, she's upset again." She thought for a moment. "And another thing—Carly's really getting *mean*. The way she's treating Callan . . . " *Not to mention some of the things she's said to me*, she added to herself.

"Is that all you see?" Marta asked. "Just the way she's acting toward other people?"

"Well, she also has this crazy thing about losing weight. It's like she can't see how skinny she is. She keeps saying she just has to get rid of those last five pounds, but when I saw her changing last night . . . it's like she's nothing but bones. You can't tell 'cause she always wears those huge T-shirts, but without her clothes on, you wouldn't believe how thin she looks." Nikki almost kept going and told them what had happened on the path yesterday, but something stopped her.

Marta was nodding as she talked. "Well, I think you've hit on it, Nik. Her parents are seeing the same changes. And noticing how she doesn't ever want to eat anymore. They're afraid she's becoming anorexic."

Anorexic. The word echoed in Nikki's mind, confirming her own darkest suspicions. But Marta was still talking.

"Carly didn't even want to go to the house at Lake Michigan this summer, and you know how she's always loved spending summers there. She begged to stay with her aunt in Chicago instead. She said it was because she wanted to keep her job at The Gap, but her parents think there's a lot more going on than she's saying."

Like Jeremy? Nikki thought.

"So when her parents heard you were coming with me to Virginia, Nikki, they thought it would be good for Carly to get away from Chicago and friends there who might be influencing her. They were just hoping things would get back to normal without having to confront her. But from what I'm seeing since we picked up Carly, I think it's time we talk to her. And Phyllis agrees."

The picture of Carly's white face when Nikki had tried to talk to her yesterday flashed before Nikki's eyes. The thought of what could happen if both Dr. Phyllis and Aunt Marta confronted Carly made Nikki go cold all over.

"Look," she said, trying to sound reasonable, "I don't think you understand how upset Carly gets when you tell her she's doing something wrong. I tried to talk to her yesterday, and it didn't go well at all. I think you need to wait a little longer—not make too big a deal of it with her."

Dr. Phyllis turned her glance on Nikki again, but this time there was no smile. "It's hard to imagine making too big a deal of something that could kill her."

Nikki squirmed inwardly beneath Dr. Phyllis's steady gaze. Finally, she said, "Maybe we're all just assuming it's anorexia and we're way off base, you know? Maybe there's something else wrong." But the words sounded lame even to her own ears.

"Nik, what problem have you ever solved by pretending it isn't there or by running from it?" Aunt Marta said. "You know as well as I do that you only solve a problem by turning around and facing it."

Nikki looked from her aunt to Dr. Phyllis and back

again. "Yeah, I suppose you're right. I guess I better go get ready for church." She got to her feet slowly and opened the screen door, then turned back toward the older women. "I think Carly would listen better to me than to someone else. Could you just give me a couple days? Let me try to talk to her first?"

Marta and Phyllis looked at each other, then back at Nikki. "We can wait a few days, but it can't be long, Nikki," Marta said.

Nikki's mind was already revising the conversation as she climbed the stairs to the bedroom she and Carly shared. *They're probably making this into a much more serious problem than it is. So Carly hides some junk food under her bed. It's not really all that strange when you think about it. Lots of people keep stuff in their rooms for a late-night snack.*

On the other hand, Carly had admitted last night that she was losing weight too fast and exercising too much.

And she promised to stop.

A promise she's already broken, Nikki's mind added.

There could be reasons she went running this morning. Reasons I don't know anything about. I have to give her the benefit of the doubt.

Nikki pulled open the bedroom door, then stopped dead in the doorway. Carly, who must have come back in through the kitchen from her run, stood in front of the dresser, an open bag of potato chips in her hands. Confusion showed on her face, along with a mixture of fear and anger, and what she did next reminded Nikki of a little girl. In a flash, Carly whipped the bag behind her back, then looked at Nikki defiantly, her chin high in the air.

❦ Eleven ❦

CARLY'S BROWN EYES STARED into Nikki's blue ones. For a second everything seemed to freeze, until Nikki stepped all the way into the room and closed the door behind her.

Carly took a step backward, then spoke, her brown eyes flashing. "Spying on me again, huh?"

The unfairness of it broke Nikki's spell.

"Wait a minute, Carly. You know that's not fair. I was worried sick about you when I woke up and you were gone." Nikki crossed to her bed and dropped down, her back against the headboard and her arms cradling a pillow in front of her like a shield. "You promised you'd stop exercising all the time."

"So I changed my mind. I had to, okay? Besides, I only ran for a half hour this morning, so get off my case, would you?"

Carly turned and grabbed clean underwear out of the dresser, banging and shoving drawers with far more force than necessary. When she grabbed her robe and started toward the door, Nikki knew it was now or never.

"Wait a minute, Carly."

Carly stopped and turned.

"We were talking this morning. About . . . about eating . . . problems. You know what I mean?" Nikki asked.

Carly's eyes narrowed. "No, I don't. So what's your point, Nik? I have to go take a shower."

Nikki sighed. This was going to be harder than she'd thought. "Well, we were wondering if, uh, if you . . . might be, like, having one of those problems. You know?"

But Carly was not about to be cornered that easily. "No, I *don't* know. And who is *we*, anyway? I'd like to know exactly who it is you feel so free to discuss me with." Instead of waiting for an answer, she rushed on. "Oh, but I forgot—that's what good friends do, isn't it? Talk about you behind your back. With other people who have no business knowing stuff about you, like that stupid Callan."

"No, it *wasn't* that stupid Callan!" Nikki shot back, then realized what she'd said. "Now look—you've got me doing it, too! Callan isn't stupid at all. What is it with you and Callan, anyway? I think the real reason you're so mean to him is that you just don't like the way he looks, isn't that right, Carly? You can insult him and be mean to him because if he doesn't look good, he doesn't matter to you. All you care about these days is how people look, Carly Allen. And *that's* what's really stupid!"

Twin red spots flamed high on Carly's cheeks, bright against her light skin, and even in the tension of the moment, the thought ran through Nikki's mind that exactly the same thing happened to Jeff when he got upset. But the thought was lost in the loud slam of the bedroom door as Carly left.

Nikki sat perfectly still for several moments, staring straight ahead. Then, with a long sigh, she hugged the pillow tighter and leaned her forehead against it. *Well, you*

*certainly blew that one. You not only let Carly get you totally off
the subject, you yelled at her for calling Callan stupid and then
turned around and called her the same thing.*

She shook her head back and forth against the cool,
smooth pillowcase. Carly—the old Carly—would have responded so differently to such a show of temper. There
would have been a raised eyebrow, a grin, then in rapid fire,
"Have you ever considered teaching a course in winning
friends and influencing people, Nik? Or maybe a job in public relations?" They would have laughed together then, and
it would have been over. Just like that.

But that was a hundred years ago, and this was now.

Nikki felt the tears drip down her cheeks and wet the
pillow beneath her face. *I'm sorry, Lord,* she began to pray.
*All I've done is fuss and worry about this, and I never once thought
to ask You for help. But it's obvious I'm not doing any good on my
own, so I'm asking You now. Please help Carly with her problem.
And please help me, too. Help me figure out how to be there for her.*

But even in the middle of her prayer, she couldn't shut
out the nagging question that kept sounding in her mind.
Finally, she slipped to her knees beside Carly's bed and
looked underneath it. *What happened to all those donuts, anyway? Nobody could've eaten all those in one day. Not unless—*
Nikki pushed the thought away.

Nikki didn't wait around to borrow the yellow dress
after Carly left. She threw on a flowered skirt and a sleeveless knit top, stuck her bare feet into sandals and took off
down the steps. There was no way she was going to risk
running into Carly.

The ride to church was not easy. Dr. Phyllis suggested
they all go together in her blue Skylark, and Nikki felt a
twinge of conscience when she and Carly both insisted that
Callan sit between them in the backseat. He glanced back

and forth from one face to the other, then rolled his eyes and slid awkwardly into the middle seat.

Nikki couldn't be sure, but she thought she heard him mutter, "Gives me a whole new respect for shuttle diplomacy," as he did so.

Dr. Phyllis and Marta began debating the origins of the folk song Annie had sung on the tape from the festival.

"Sing that last verse, would you, Callan?" Dr. Phyllis said. "So Marta can see what I mean?"

Callan obliged, then the next thing Nikki knew, her aunt and Dr. Phyllis and Callan ended up singing crazy children's choruses, laughing hard as Dr. Phyllis drove.

Nikki and Carly sat in silence, staring straight ahead. Callan kept looking back and forth from one girl to the other, and Nikki felt more and more that she was acting as immature as some of the preschoolers she baby-sat. And the more childish she felt, the angrier she got about the whole situation—especially at Carly.

It was after lunch when things were finally resolved. Nikki announced distinctly that she was going out to the barn to check on the kittens, sure that Carly would stay as far away as possible. Instead, Nikki barely had time to corner Patches and pick her up when she heard the rustle of hay from the doorway. She turned so quickly that Patches jumped from her hands and disappeared into one of the empty stalls. Carly stood at the door, looking sheepish.

She held her hands up. "Okay, okay, I surrender. You were right, Nikki. I *am* having kind of a . . . a . . . problem. About eating. But it's not what you think, all right?"

She waited till Nikki nodded, then went on. "I mean, it's not like what they show on those TV movies, like I have an eating disorder or something. I told you yesterday, I've just been trying to lose those last five pounds." She hung her head. "But I meant what I told you yesterday—that I'd start eating right and stop exercising so much. I just . . . when I got up this morning, I just . . . *needed* to go running. And when I got back, I was hungry, you know? So I was gonna have some chips. I promise, Nik, I really wasn't lying to you yesterday. I meant what I said. And I'm okay now. I just blew it this morning, that's all. I only need a little more will-power, you know? I can conquer this, I know I can."

Nikki knew this was as close as Carly would ever come to apologizing, and with a sudden fierce gladness that Carly had come to her senses, she closed the distance between them with four long steps and hugged Carly briefly.

"That's great, Carly. I'm so relieved to hear it."

Carly hugged her back, a little awkwardly, then said quickly, "Come on, let's walk over to Tory and Marissa's."

The walk was totally different this time. Carly cracked joke after joke and kept Nikki laughing most of the way. She seemed so normal again that Nikki whispered a silent prayer as they walked. *Thank you, Lord, that Carly's finally back.*

The Holsom bread truck was missing today, and in its place sat a blue van. There was rust around the edges of the driver's-side door, and the door itself was patterned with a network of dents where other doors had banged against it over the years. But there was also a carefully lettered sign on the side that read, "Barker's Electronics—Computers & Small Appliances."

Mrs. Barker's face lit up when she answered the door. "Nikki and Carly! Come on in." She shut the door behind them and led them toward the kitchen. "Tory's downstairs in the computer room with her father. But Marissa's gone off somewhere with Annie. She came over on her horse an hour or so ago, and Marissa took Shiloh and left with her." She picked up a half-peeled potato from the cutting board and began working at the rest of the peel with a small paring knife. "She should be back any time, though." Her lips tightened in a thin, straight line. "I know Annie's father doesn't like her away from the house for long."

Tory appeared in the basement doorway. "Hi! I heard you guys talking."

Nikki noted that her hair was arranged in a French braid again, though a clumsy one she'd obviously tried to do herself. They went back to the girls' bedroom, where Carly took out Tory's braid and showed her once more how to do it.

When she finished, Carly said, "Well, we just came by to say hi and see how you and Marissa were doing. I guess we'd better get back."

But Carly hung back as the girls walked down the hallway. She hesitated a moment, until Nikki was almost to the kitchen, then called, "You go ahead, Nik. I'll be right there."

Nikki turned and saw Carly slip into the bathroom. As she waited in the small entryway, uneasiness stirred inside her as she remembered the Barkers had a scale in there.

Marissa's arrival on Shiloh just then was a welcome interruption to Nikki's thoughts. Marissa smiled at her and slid down off the big horse, gathering the reins in one hand and leading Shiloh toward the barn, but there was a worried look in her eyes.

"Hi, Nikki. Do you want to come to the barn with me while I take care of Shiloh?"

They walked together to Shiloh's stall, and Nikki rubbed his soft muzzle while Marissa unbuckled the saddle.

"You know my friend Annie?" Marissa said. "The one you recorded at the festival on Friday night?"

Nikki nodded. "Sure. She's got an awesome voice. I told you Aunt Marta's really excited about her. Dr. Phyllis is, too."

"I know. They called her dad and said they wanted to take Annie to talk with some music professor at the university about having lessons."

"Good," Nikki answered. "So what's the problem?"

"Her dad, as usual. He went ballistic. Annie said it was pretty awful, even for him."

Nikki turned to face the younger girl, puzzled. "But why? This could mean a really big chance for her to get great training."

"*I* know that, and *you* know that, Nikki. And Annie really wants to. But her dad said—well, I guess I better not repeat *exactly* what he said, but he told her that if she's that good she should be talking to an agent, not to people like your aunt. Or people at the university. He says people like that just want to use her. For free."

Nikki looked at her in disbelief. "You're kidding, right?"

Marissa shook her head vehemently. "That's what he said—'This is just their way of getting to use you for free.'"

"Which means *he* wants to use her to make money, right?"

Marissa shrugged. "Nobody would dare say that to him."

"So what happened? I mean, did he change his mind?"

Marissa rolled her eyes. "You don't know him very well, do you?"

Nikki thought back to the scene at the stop sign on their first day in town. *Better than I want to!*

Marissa went on. "When Annie's dad says something, he *never* backs down. My mother says that since Annie's mom died, he's turned into the most pigheaded man she's ever seen. Meaner than a snake, too." Her voice cracked on the word *snake*, and she looked down, concentrating hard on the toe of her sneaker, drawing a line with it in the light coating of hay dust on the concrete floor. "She's my best friend, Nikki. And she's in a big mess. When her dad gets mad, there's no telling what might happen." She turned to face Nikki. "You probably don't know how it feels to have a friend in trouble, but believe me, it doesn't feel very good!"

Nikki closed her eyes and wished she *didn't* know how it felt. She tried hard not to think about Carly coming all the way over there, pretending she wanted to visit Tory and Marissa. And probably all just so she could use the scale. She tried not to let her mind replay all Dr. Phyllis had said that morning about eating disorders.

"Don't worry. I believe you, Marissa."

"Well, is there some way you can help? I don't want Annie to miss this chance to study with some big university professor. She really wants to be a singer—just not the kind her dad wants her to be."

Nikki hesitated. "Well, he sure wouldn't listen to anything I say." *Especially if he recognizes me!* she added to herself. "But maybe I could talk to Dr. Phyllis and my aunt. They'll have some ideas."

Marissa could hardly control her excitement. "Would you do that? Right away—like this afternoon?"

Nikki nodded. "Sure. I don't know what they'll come up with, but I know they'll think of something."

Back at the house, the older women, sitting at a kitchen table piled high with music scores, audio tapes, and manuscript pages, listened indignantly as Nikki recounted what Marissa had told her. Carly punctuated Nikki's comments with her own nods and sighs.

Dr. Phyllis pursed her lips and leaned against the back of her chair, arms crossed over her chest. "There he was, talking so politely to us on the phone, then saying those hateful things behind our backs!" she muttered, shaking her head.

Aunt Marta slapped the manuscript in her hands down

on the table. "It's the most ridiculous—not to mention *insulting*—thing I've ever heard. He thinks we want to use Annie? To make money for ourselves?" She pushed back her chair with a loud scrape and starting pacing.

Nikki and Carly stole a quick glance at one another, and Carly made a face. They both knew someone was in for trouble when Aunt Marta started pacing.

"Can you believe this?" Marta said. "We try to help a child who's probably never going to get a better opportunity, and her father—her own father—stands in the way." She broke off and whirled to face Dr. Phyllis. "So let's go talk to him in person. We can make him see reason. Come on." She motioned to the door, but before Dr. Phyllis got to her feet, Nikki began to speak.

"Um, Aunt Marta?"

Her aunt glanced back over her shoulder at Nikki, one eyebrow raised, waiting. "Yes?"

"That may not be the best idea. . . ."

"What are you talking about?"

"Going to see Annie's father," Nikki answered.

Marta turned, waiting impatiently. After Nikki hesitated a few seconds, Marta said, "Perhaps you'd like to tell me why?"

"Well . . . I just thought you should know who Annie's father is before you go."

Marta's hand was on the doorknob by now. "Okay," she said with exaggerated patience. "And just who *is* Annie's father?"

Nikki and Carly glanced at each other.

"Remember when we got here on Friday?" Nikki said. "When we were at the stop sign and Carly—"

Carly glared at Nikki and quickly shook her head.

"—well, remember that guy who yelled at us?"

Marta stared at them for a moment, then her shoulders

sagged. *"That's* Annie's father?"

Nikki and Carly nodded slowly, in tandem, as though their heads were both attached to the same string.

Marta's hand fell from the doorknob, and her resolve appeared to vanish.

Dr. Phyllis, meanwhile, sat forward in her chair, listening intently. "Hmmm. Now why do I get the feeling that I don't have all the information here?" she asked. "Would one of you three like to let me in on what's going on?"

❦ *Twelve* ❦

CARLY AND NIKKI BOTH STARTED TALKING at once, with Marta chiming in to clarify details. When they had finished and Dr. Phyllis had managed to sort out the whole story, her faced turned somber.

"This probably isn't going to further our cause with him much," she said. "Leonard Slayton may not impress you as being very smart, but he's got a memory like the proverbial elephant. And I doubt he's ever given much thought to the idea of 'forgive and forget.' "

"Great," Marta murmured. "That's just great." She walked back to the table and sank into her chair. "Now what do we do?"

Dr. Phyllis regarded Marta evenly, but Nikki could see the hint of a smile in her eyes. "But I thought you were so anxious to go talk some sense into him."

Marta put her elbows on the table and leaned her chin on her hands. "Phyllis, after that performance he gave in the middle of the road the other day, I think talking sense to him would be Mission: Impossible. You just said yourself that, in light of my experience with him, reasoning with him probably wouldn't help our cause. I have this sneaking suspicion he still has plenty to say to me. And he'd be venting before we'd ever even get to the subject of Annie."

"But we have to do something," Nikki put in.

Marta looked at her, furrows etched deeply into her forehead. "You have a suggestion?"

"Well, not exactly. But don't you always tell me to stand up to whatever I'm most scared of?"

Marta winced and dropped her forehead into her hands. "Oh, brother. This is the part where my own words come back to haunt me, right?"

Nikki shrugged, half apologetically, half laughing. "Sorry, Aunt Marta, but that *is* what you've said—about a million times, if I'm counting right."

"It's time to take my own medicine, I guess." Marta got to her feet. "Well, Phyllis, what do you think? If we go and talk to Annie's father, is it likely to make things better or worse for her?"

Dr. Phyllis got to her feet beside Marta. "Maybe a little of both," she said. "We'll probably have to get through the *worse* part before we get to the *better*. But that's not the issue. The issue is that we have to go and do all we can. And I think we need to talk to him before the festival announces the contest winner tonight, because I think Annie stands a real chance of winning. If she does, all the publicity hounds and agents will be knocking at Len Slayton's door." She picked up her purse from the counter beside the refrigerator and headed for the hall. "Just let me tell Callan where we're going, and I'll be right out to the car."

Neither Carly or Nikki had any desire to see Leonard Slayton again and were glad to stay out of the confrontation. After Marta's car disappeared down the driveway, Carly announced she was going upstairs to take a nap.

Nikki went to the wide front porch and made her way

through the wicker furniture to the porch swing. A nap sounded like a fine idea to her, too. She stretched out on the flowered cushions where she could see over the sprawling front lawn and the driveway to the blue line of hills in the distance. She thought about Dr. Phyllis turning to her early that morning and asking, "Do you pray, Nikki?"

Which is what I should be doing right now, she thought. But as she began, asking the Lord first, as she always did, for Evan's well-being, the screen door opened with its usual loud creak.

Callan followed the same route she'd taken earlier between pieces of wicker furniture, though his movements were much slower and accompanied by the steady click of his crutches. When he got to the rocker across from the swing, he dropped into it and grinned at her.

Nikki smiled back but couldn't help feeling sad as she watched him. The gray plastic cuffs of the forearm crutches looked for an instant like handcuffs to her, trapping Callan in their grip. Then the idea faded as he propped the crutches against the wicker end table and settled back in the rocker.

"Where's your sidekick?" he asked.

"Taking a nap," Nikki answered. She hesitated, then asked a question in return. "So is it a relief or a disappointment that Carly's not here?"

Callan looked at her and gave a self-deprecating laugh. "Okay, so you've noticed. And you're right, I *do* think Carly's pretty, and I don't mind it when she's around." He made a face. "Her personality could stand a little work, but—"

"She's not usually like this, Callan," Nikki broke in. "Normally she's as nice as she is pretty. At least, she used to be."

"Yeah, well, I sure haven't seen *that* side of her yet. But you can't help noticing her, that's for sure." His gaze followed Nikki's quick glance at his legs. "It doesn't make any difference, Nik. Muscular dystrophy is just something I *have*, not something that stops me from being a guy."

"Oh, I didn't mean—" Nikki stopped in confusion, her face red.

Callan's voice was kind. "I know. And don't feel bad. It's just that people sometimes think a disability defines who you are, and maybe in some ways it does—on the outside. But I'm not disabled on the inside. I'm just like any other guy.

"But anyway, back to Carly. I think there's a lot more going on with her than what you see on the outside," Callan added.

"Actually, I think she's doing better, Callan. She's been struggling with some things—losing weight and all—but she's going to be okay now." Nikki hesitated, then couldn't resist adding, "Dr. Phyllis and my aunt are trying to make a big deal of how she's acting, but I think they're blowing it a little out of proportion."

"Blowing what out of proportion?"

"Oh, they're talking about *eating disorders.*"

"You don't think it's a problem?"

"Well, yeah, but not like they do. I just think their minds are full of worse-case scenarios, you know? Dr. Phyllis even talked about how some girls die from anorexia. . . ."

"Some *do* die from anorexia, Nikki."

"I know that, Callan! I'm just saying, it won't happen to Carly. She doesn't have *that* kind of problem."

Callan rocked silently for a minute, his eyebrows raised.

"She doesn't, Callan. Believe me, I know. She realizes she wasn't eating very well and that she was exercising way too much. She told me that herself, and she's going to stop, okay? You don't know her the way I do. Carly's a very *in-control* person, and if she says she's going to stop, she will."

Callan kept on rocking, then looked up. "Isn't being in control the whole issue?"

"What do you mean?"

"I read that for a lot of people who have eating disorders, being in control is what it's all about." Callan leaned forward, his hands together between his knees. "Not eating, or eating in specific ways, or eating and then throwing up—they're all supposed to be ways the person tries to take control of his or her life."

"Oh, right!" Nikki said. "Some control."

"No, I'm serious," Callan insisted. "We learned about it in psych class last year. We had this lady come in who had been bulimic and almost died."

Nikki stood up and stretched, trying to cover her uneasiness. "Yeah, well, if you knew Carly, you'd know *taking control* is not the issue. I mean, nobody's ever been more in control than her. She's made up her mind to do something, and she'll follow through. And once she does, I'm sure her moods will go right back to normal. You might even get to know her the way she really is, Callan."

Nikki turned and headed for the door, and Callan fitted his crutches in place beneath his elbows.

"Nikki?" he said, as she reached for the handle of the screen door.

"What?" she asked.

"Just don't be too let down if she doesn't do exactly what she told you."

"Callan, you're not listening. Carly said—"

Callan's eyes came up to meet hers then, and he looked at her for a moment before he spoke. "That's what people usually do when they're trying to hide something, isn't it? I mean, people can *say* anything. It's what they *do* that counts."

Nikki held the screen door open for Callan, then

followed him inside, watching as he turned toward the studio and made his way down the hall.

Nikki went slowly upstairs. She opened the bedroom door and tiptoed inside, trying to see whether Carly, who lay on top of the thin cotton bedspread with her back to the door, was awake or not. She was halfway around the bed to check when she saw Carly's shoulders shake.

"Carly! You're not asleep, are you?" she demanded.

Again there came the same slight shake of the shoulders and a tiny crackle. Nikki swooped down suddenly and gave the pillow a terrific jerk. Carly flopped over, her face red from silent laughter. She sat up in one fluid, graceful motion.

"Fooled you! And look," she reached down by her side to show Nikki the bag of baby carrots. "See? I'm eating! And it's *good stuff*, okay? I'm taking care of myself now. You want some?"

Carly held the open bag toward her friend, and Nikki climbed up onto the foot of the bed and sat cross-legged.

The next half hour was so much like "old times" that Nikki could hardly believe she'd worried about Carly. By the time they finished talking and heard Marta's car pull into the drive, the carrot bag was entirely empty. Nikki was a little surprised to see that, since she knew she'd eaten only a few of the carrots. But that didn't seem like any big deal. After all, who could eat too many carrots?

What mattered was that Carly was back to normal, chattering on and on about Jeff and things at home and the phone call she'd gotten from her mother and father that morning.

So why couldn't Nikki shake her uneasiness?

Nikki was waiting in the doorway when Dr. Phyllis and Aunt Marta drove up. Callan had heard the car and got to the kitchen in time to hear their whole report. Only Carly came in late because she'd had to make another "quick trip to the bathroom" first.

Nikki could tell from the older women's faces that the meeting with Annie's father had not gone the way they would have liked. Aunt Marta stepped into the kitchen and laid her purse carefully on the kitchen table, then spoke in a tightly controlled voice.

"He may be the single most unreasonable man I have ever met. No, make that the single most unreasonable *person*," she corrected herself.

Aunt Marta's not used to losing arguments, Nikki thought. *She's so logical and articulate that she can usually make everyone around her see things her way.* But obviously not this time.

Even Dr. Phyllis seemed subdued.

Carly hurried into the kitchen. She looked from face to face before she said, "I guess things didn't go too well, huh?"

Dr. Phyllis opened the freezer door and peered at the packages stacked on the shelves. "I think that's probably an understatement," she said dryly.

Aunt Marta pulled out a chair and sat down, combing her hair back off her face with both hands as she always did when she was upset. A section of her bangs spiked straight up, but she was oblivious to anything but the subject at hand.

"I talked to that man till I was nearly blue in the face, and it didn't do a bit of good," she began. "I told him I teach at Indiana University, that I'm writing this book for Sotheby Press—even he recognized a name that big—and that we wouldn't receive any money for what we want to do for Annie. Putting her in touch with the teachers at the university here would be the best thing that ever happened to her, musically. But no, none of that was good enough for Leonard Slayton."

"What's his problem?" Carly asked. "What kind of parent wouldn't want what's best for his own kid?"

Nikki looked at Carly, and her eyes narrowed. She tried not to remember the day her own parents had tricked her into going to the abortion doctor. *Boy, have you got a lot to learn,* she wanted to tell Carly. *But then, with the parents you've got, you'll never face the kind of stuff I had to confront. The stuff Annie deals with.*

"The man doesn't seem to think about Annie at all," Aunt Marta was saying, "except about what she can do for him. Apparently, he's not only worried that we intend to act as agents that would make bundles of money off her—he keeps going on and on about 'middlemen'—but he's also worried that if she does start having lessons and meeting other people who want to help her, she won't be around to cook his meals and wash his clothes and do his dishes. Can you believe this guy?"

Marta's elbows rested on the table and her hands, clasped in front of her, thudded down on the table. "Well, let me tell you, this isn't over yet. There's no way I'm going to stand by and let him do this."

Dr. Phyllis put a package of meat into the microwave and hit Defrost, then turned to face them. "I'm afraid there's not a thing you can do about it," she said to Marta.

"Excuse me?" Marta said, more sharply than normal.

Dr. Phyllis sat down across the table from her and spoke quietly. "Marta, listen. You know as well as I do that if a person is beyond reasoning with, there's no way you can change him."

Marta's lips pressed together tightly, but she didn't say a word.

The older woman smiled across the table and spoke in

a gentle voice. "I know you care about Annie. About seeing her get the training she needs and everything—"

"It's not just that," Marta burst out. "Look at how she has to live. If it weren't for that flower bed she's so proud of, the place would be without any kind of beauty. It's really just a shack. It's pretty obvious that whatever money Leonard Slayton *does* make, he doesn't spend it on his daughter. He's just drinking it all up, isn't he?"

Dr. Phyllis nodded. "I'm afraid so."

"Phyllis! The girl's a born musician. A natural. People like that don't come along every day. And he can't see beyond the nose on his face, beyond signing her up to sing in some local bar to make him more money to drink up. So I ask you—why do we have to stand by and *watch?*"

"We don't," Dr. Phyllis answered calmly.

Marta looked really frustrated now. Nikki held her breath, waiting.

"You just *said* we couldn't change him, Phyllis Brummels."

"I know."

"Well, then? What do you mean, 'We don't'?"

The microwave timer beeped, and Dr. Phyllis got up to remove the meat she was defrosting. "I think you're forgetting, Marta, that we're not the only ones involved in this situation. There is someone else interested in what happens to Annie. Remember?" She unwrapped the hamburger and held it over the sink so the red juice could drip down the drain. "You know who I'm talking about—He's able to change anybody."

Nikki wondered if Marta would be offended that she'd been corrected. But her aunt relaxed against the chair back and said, "You're absolutely right."

After a moment, Marta looked around at Callan, Carly, and Nikki. "Looks as though I left out the most important part of the equation, doesn't it? Would you mind if we prayed for Annie and her father right now?"

Marta, Dr. Phyllis, and Callan left immediately after dinner for another night of interviews and appointments at the last night of the Shenandoah Folk Festival. Carly and Nikki planned to go in later, after the traffic died down, to hear the contest winner announced. They cleaned up the kitchen after dinner, checked on the kittens out in the barn, and worked their way through three more of Carly's makeover quizzes. They'd been surfing through the television channels for 10 minutes or so, with no success, when Carly burst out suddenly, "I know what we can do! Come on, we can leave early."

Nikki hit the Mute button and looked up at her. "Oh, yeah? Why?"

"We'll go into town and get you new makeup! We can put into practice all the stuff you just learned in that last quiz." She looked immensely pleased with herself for thinking of it. "You know you need it, Nik. And there was a drugstore right next to the Piggly Wiggly. Come on."

"But why, Carly? I like the makeup I'm using now."

"Nikki." Carly put her hands on her hips. "What good is learning all this if you don't *use* it? I've tried and tried to explain this to you." She sounded exasperated. "You've got to have the right makeup. Everybody can tell you're out-of-date when you're still using last year's stuff. Purples are in this year, and all your eyeshadow is that old blue stuff."

Nikki sighed and switched off the TV. There was no way she would win this battle—she knew that from experience. But having the "old" Carly back made Nikki glad enough to go along with just about anything.

"Let me go find the car keys," she said finally.

Carly steered them through another quiz on the ride into

town. Nikki was still puzzling over the last question as she braked at the stop sign. Her glance fell on the chain-link fence around the deserted gas station. There, stuck into one of the openings, was another bouquet.

"Look at that, Carly," she said, nodding toward the fence. "There's a new bouquet over there, just like Callan said there would be."

"Uh-huh," Carly murmured, without even looking up. "Try to keep your mind on the question, Nik, so we can get finished before we get to the store. Now listen again: 'How long can you safely use eye makeup once it's been opened?' The answer is six months. See? I bet you didn't even know there *was* a time limit, did you? You know all that blue stuff I told you to get rid of? Well, here's why!" she said as she held up the magazine.

"Right, Carly," Nikki answered, pulling her mind away from the bouquet.

"Okay," Carly said, totalling up the score, "that takes care of that. Now—" she pulled a letter from her parents out of her purse and began to write on the back of the envelope "—let's make a list of everything you need so we don't forget anything. We'll do shadows in mauve and purple—you know, those three-packs with the highlighting colors that coordinate—and a new liner." She turned and inspected Nikki's face intently. "I think a brown-black liner and mascara. Plain black is too harsh. And outdated, of course," she added hurriedly.

Of course. We certainly wouldn't want to be outdated, Nikki answered back in her own mind. *Why, that'd be just about the most terrible thing anybody could think of, wouldn't it?* And then she immediately felt sorry. *Straighten up, Nikki. Carly's trying her best to do something nice for you and you're thinking up snide remarks.*

Still, it bothered her how Carly always had to be

changing things, improving them. It wasn't so much that she wanted to make things better. *It's almost a compulsion, as though no matter what she does, she can never change other people—or herself—enough to be satisfied.*

Thirteen

THE NEXT MORNING WAS THE DAY Tory and Marissa could finally claim their kittens, and they were there bright and early. Nikki was still moving slowly after being out late at the festival the night before. She didn't know whether to frown or smile at the way Annie's face had looked when Andy Allender had been proclaimed the winner of the "Beauty Contest"—frown because she thought Annie must be disappointed, or smile because losing might take off some of the pressure with her father.

Now, sitting on the front step, Nikki eyed the heavily overcast sky and began tying her running shoes while Carly fussed with her hair. Just then, Tory came bounding across the yard.

"Hey! We get to take our kittens home today! How are you guys? I didn't think you'd even be awake yet!" she yelled, her words coming in bursts as each foot pounded the ground.

"Yeah, well, don't believe everything you see," Nikki muttered, tightening her shoestrings. "We're not awake yet. At least, one of us isn't."

Nikki had never enjoyed jogging in the summer heat, and as a result, she hadn't been for a couple of months now. *Time to get back into the habit*, Nikki thought, trying to tell herself that was why she'd dragged herself out of bed. But she knew that wasn't the only reason. Carly had insisted she was just going for a normal run, like everyone else did.

"Stop worrying!" she'd ordered. "Nothing's going to happen, Nik. You don't have to be my mother, you know!"

But the thought of Carly's heart skipping all those beats made pictures in Nikki's head she didn't like: Carly fainting somewhere out on the trail in the middle of nowhere, hitting her head on a log . . . Carly lying dead on the path a mile away . . .

Nikki shook her head to clear away the thoughts.

"Get with the program, you old stick-in-the-mud," said the very-much-alive Carly. She prodded Nikki with one sneaker-clad foot, the blue and white laces dangling over the side. Then she raised her foot to the porch railing and began her usual series of stretches. She bent her head to meet her knee, and her shiny blonde hair fell forward to hide her face. "You've been sleeping in every morning. It's about time you got up and got some exercise," she said from behind the curtain of hair.

Marissa came into view then, lugging a cardboard cat carrier. But Tory's excitement about the kittens seemed to take a backseat as she fixed her attention on Carly's every move.

"Remember I told you I always wanted to jog?" Tory asked finally as Carly straightened up.

Carly grinned at her. "So what's stopping you?" She glanced at Tory's feet before she leaned into another stretch. "Those may not be the best jogging shoes, but at least they're sneakers. Come with us."

"What about the kittens?" asked Marissa, who had set

the cat carrier down on the sidewalk and was now sitting on the porch step beside Nikki.

Carly thought for a second, then shrugged. "After we're done jogging, Nikki and I will drive you home. You can't lug cats up over that path in the carrier, anyway. They'll be scared to death from getting bumped around that way. Don't you think it'd be better if we drove them, Nik?"

"It's fine with me," Nikki answered. "I just thought Tory was more anxious than that to get those kittens home."

Marissa spoke in a low voice beside her. "Not as anxious as she is to become a perfect little Carly clone."

"What'd you say?" Tory demanded. "Was it something about me?"

Marissa ignored her, and Tory responded angrily, "Well, it better not have been, that's all I can say!"

"I'm scared. I'm shaking," Marissa said in a bored tone, without even a glance in her sister's direction.

"I'm gonna tell Mom—" Tory began, but Carly cut in.

"Oh, come on, you two! Call a truce. Why don't you come with us, too, Marissa? Those shoes would work fine, I bet."

"*Marissa? Jog?*" Tory said, laughing. "You expect somebody that big to—"

"Knock it off!" Carly said. "Didn't I just tell you to call a truce?"

She began jogging across the yard toward the driveway, and they all fell in line obediently behind her.

Like always, Nikki thought, then found she had to concentrate on running. It took only a few minutes for Nikki to discover just how out of shape she'd gotten in the past few months. But she was determined to keep close to Carly, alert for any signs of . . . what?

How am I supposed to know what the signs of a heart problem would be?

Nikki sighed and kept running, watching Tory and Carly moving farther and farther ahead down the tree-lined driveway, talking and laughing effortlessly as they jogged. She and Marissa, on the other hand, talked in a kind of shorthand—blurting out two or three words only when absolutely necessary—and spent a lot of time sucking air.

Carly led them up the half-mile driveway to the road, then back again. By now, Nikki and Marissa had fallen 50 feet behind, so they met Carly and Tory face to face on their way back.

"Come on, you slowpokes!" Carly chided as they went past.

Tory grinned and waved triumphantly.

When they got back to the house, Nikki thought, *That makes one mile*. She expected Carly to turn and make the circuit again. Instead, Nikki watched as her friend headed off across the yard toward the path to the Barkers'.

"Hey! Where're you taking us?" Nikki yelled, stopping for a moment in the drive.

Carly waved the slower joggers on with one hand and yelled back over her shoulder, "Just to the top and back. We'll see how fit you really are!"

Nikki and Marissa glanced at one another in dismay, then Nikki hollered after Carly, "I could save you a lot of trouble and just *tell* you."

Marissa sighed and slumped onto the porch steps. "Come on, we can wait here till they get back, Nikki." She motioned to the step beside her, but Nikki shook her head.

"I can't, Marissa." She started off after Carly and Tory, her calf muscles beginning to ache.

"Why?" Marissa said. "Why do you have to go with them?"

Nikki didn't answer. She couldn't tell Marissa her worries about Carly or about her determination to keep an eye on her—Carly would kill her if she did.

It took sheer perseverance to keep putting one foot ahead of the other. She couldn't believe Carly would try to run up a steep path like this one. *But then, who knows what Carly will do these days?*

As the slant of the path grew sharper, Nikki's pace slowed more and more. Even Tory's energy seemed to be flagging now, and she was falling behind. But if Nikki was sure of anything about the younger girl, it was that Tory would push herself far beyond all sensible limits to be like her idol.

Nikki's real concern, though, was Carly. What if she kept showing off this way and had another spell with her heart? *It isn't exactly the kind of thing you expect to have to think about with a friend who's 16, that's for sure.*

Nikki was all wrapped up in her thoughts, so much so that when it happened, it took a moment for her to process. She heard Carly call from far ahead, "Hey, Tory, get the lead out!" She saw Tory look up and start to yell back something Nikki couldn't hear.

The next thing she heard was a loud *snap* as Tory's right foot slid off the path.

One minute they were all jogging up the path. The next, Tory was on the ground, writhing and grabbing at her right leg.

Nikki was at the girl's side in seconds, shouting for Carly to come back. Dropping to her knees beside Tory, Nikki saw at once what had happened. The groundhog holes Marissa had warned them about, the ones so likely to fell a horse, had gotten Tory instead. Damp dirt still lay around the hole, showing how recently it had been dug, and Tory had had more important things on her mind than watching where she was going.

"I was just . . . trying to . . . catch up . . . with . . . Carly," she gasped as Nikki smoothed the hair, damp from sweat, back off her forehead and tried to think what on earth she was supposed to do next. "I just . . . wanted to run . . . as fast . . . as she did," Tory continued, clutching at her leg. Her face was twisted in pain, and tears were running down across the freckles.

She looked at Nikki through squinting eyes, and sobbed, "Oh, Nikki, my leg hurts *so bad!* Nikki, please help me." Her voice rose in a high-pitched wail. *"Do something!"*

Fourteen

HELPING TORY TOOK UP THE REST of the day.

Carly had reached the top of the hill and turned to come back before she noticed Nikki's yelling. She sprinted down the path, calling, "What's going on? What's wrong with Tory?"

But when she reached them, Nikki couldn't keep the anger out of her reply. "She was trying to keep up with *you*, Carly! You, the big show-off runner, and look where it got her! Since you're so fast, *you* run and get Dr. Phyllis and my aunt and call for an ambulance."

Carly stared at her, and Nikki bit her lip to keep from saying more as she turned back to Tory.

It seemed to take hours for help to get there and then to get Tory back to where the ambulance was parked on the lawn beside the path, maneuvered as close to the foot of the hill as the driver could get it. Finally, everyone piled into the cars, the kittens and everything else totally forgotten. They were too busy deciding that Nikki and Marta were to follow the ambulance to the hospital in Lima, Callan and Dr. Phyllis would take Marissa and go pick up Lou Barker, and they'd all meet at the emergency room.

And for most of the time, Tory kept up a constant wail that seemed to grow just slightly less intense as time went by. Nikki couldn't help wondering privately if Tory wasn't managing, even with the pain, to enjoy all the attention.

Even though Nikki had been the one who'd stayed with Tory, supporting and comforting her while Carly ran for help, it was still Carly whom Tory had begged to ride in the ambulance with her.

Naturally, Nikki thought as she climbed into her aunt's Taurus. She stared out the front window at a sky the color of lead and finally admitted to herself just how much that bothered her. Carly could be moody and downright annoying to people. But in the end, it was always Carly whom people liked best.

Nikki leaned her head against the car window. She knew God loved her. And people said she had a lot going for her, like getting good grades and being musical. But sometimes it felt as though she were trapped somehow—trapped by who she was. And while she could change some of the outward things about herself, the real her—inside—would always be just Nikki.

Is that so bad? a small voice in her head seemed to ask. Nikki sat very still, listening. *If you can trust Me with your whole eternity,* the voice went on, *isn't it strange you won't trust Me with who I've made you to be right here and now?*

Nikki swallowed. She'd never thought about it exactly that way before.

"Nikki!" Aunt Marta's voice broke into her thoughts. "Sorry to be so loud, but I called you three times and still couldn't get your attention. I didn't want to ask you for details in front of Tory, but I still don't understand why you all were running up such a steep path. That's not the kind of place Carly normally runs, is it?"

Nikki shook her head. "No. At least, I don't think so. Carly doesn't tell me much about what she does anymore, but I think she was just kind of . . . kind of goofing off, you know? And maybe showing off." She stopped, feeling disloyal.

"Showing off?" Aunt Marta sounded incredulous. "How exactly do you *show off* when you're jogging?"

Nikki shrugged. "She wasn't really jogging by that time. She was running. And telling us all to keep up with her. Tory was knocking herself out to do it, too. You know how she tries to do every single thing just like Carly."

Marta pushed on the turn signal and made a left turn, following the ambulance, then looked sideways at Nikki.

"Does that bother you, Nik?"

Wait a minute! Nikki wanted to say. *We're discussing Carly here, remember?* But it was no use trying to avoid a topic with Aunt Marta. She shrugged again, noncommittally. "A little bit. Maybe."

"Nikki," her aunt countered, "you can't let things like that eat at you. Honey, you've gone through so much this year. And you've come so far."

"That's all well and good," Nikki said, crossing her arms over her chest, "but when you come right down to it, no matter how 'far' I've come, Carly started out miles ahead of me. I mean, look at her family. Most kids I know would kill to have parents like Dr. and Mrs. Allen. And then there's her looks. Face it, Aunt Marta, Carly's got it *all*. Sometimes it's just hard to be around a person like that. It's kind of like . . . like . . . standing beside a poster of Miss America and trying to still pretend you're pretty, you know?"

Marta shook her head. "Oh, Nikki! Don't you see what's happening here? Sure, Carly's pretty and she's a very special person. But so are you, honey. You're just not seeing that because Carly's looks and figure fit the model our crazy culture says is the only one that counts."

When Nikki didn't say anything, Marta went on. "It's tough to live in a culture where looks and weight determine who's worthy and who's not. We spend our lives looking at underweight models on TV and in magazines and being told *they're* the 'normal' ones." She blew out a long sigh through pursed lips and shook her head again.

"But have you forgotten that we're worth far more than how we *look?* My significance, your significance—in the final analysis, it all comes from only one source, and that's our relationship with God." She reached across the seat with one hand and rubbed Nikki's shoulder. "We need to talk more about this later, I think, Nik. But right now, let me just tell you that, while Carly may look perfect on the outside, she's hurting from the effects of the culture, too."

Oh, right, Nikki thought. *Like I believe that.* Sometimes Aunt Marta was just too out of touch. She looked out the window and changed the subject pointedly. "When do you think this storm's going to hit?"

Marta glanced sideways again, and Nikki knew she hadn't fooled her aunt one bit. But she would play along.

"On the news, it said the hurricane was just circling around in the Caribbean, and these are the spin-off clouds we're getting. They're not sure if it's going to move back out to sea or move north up the eastern seaboard."

"Well, I hope it makes up its mind soon. This humidity's about to kill me." Nikki pulled down the sun visor and glanced in the mirror. "Not to mention this stupid frizz." She pushed back her hair, trying to straighten it out, with no success. The hair sprang right back up into curls. She gave up and pushed the visor back into place. "Look, that's got to be the hospital up there. That big red brick building."

The brake lights on the back of the ambulance lit red, and Marta slowed to follow the ambulance into a circular driveway behind it. She turned off the ignition, but before opening the door to get out of the car, she looked pointedly at her niece.

"Nikki, I just want you to tell me one thing—later, after you've had time to think about it. What about yourself do you *like?*"

The emergency room was nearly empty, so Tory was attended to almost as soon as they wheeled her in, wide-eyed and still howling, on the stretcher.

"Ow! Ow! You don't know how bad that hurts!" she shrieked as a young doctor probed her ankle. "You wouldn't believe it! You just don't *know!*" She kept it up, obviously annoying everyone who was trying to help her, until finally one of the nurses took her freckled face between her two hands—very gently, Nikki thought, given the circumstances—and said firmly, "You're right, honey, we don't. Now you be quiet so we can do our job and get you *out* of all that pain."

The emergency-room doctor continued to poke and prod, his brows knit together in a straight, dark line over his nose as he concentrated. Then he looked up and began barking instructions about X-rays and pain medication and other things Nikki didn't quite catch.

What she did hear clearly, though, after they'd wheeled Tory down the hall and into one of the examining rooms, was what the doctor told Tory's mother, who had just rushed in.

"We won't know for sure till we get the X-rays," the doctor said, "but I suspect a trimalleolar fracture of that right ankle joint. Just have a seat here, Mrs. Barker, and I'll be back as soon as we know for sure."

"But can't I see Tory? She'll be much calmer if I'm with her," Lou Barker protested.

The doctor looked around the group, frowning. "But

somebody already went with her."

The door of the examining room down the hall opened, and Nikki and the others had a moment's view of Tory on her gurney.

"Marissa's with her! Oh, good," Lou Barker said, her voice soft with relief, and after the doctor waved her on, she hurried to join her girls.

Good? Nikki thought. *The two of them are usually ready to kill each other!* But when she looked down the hall in the direction Lou Barker was heading, she saw with surprise that Tory was holding on to Marissa's hand for dear life, looking up at her intently while Marissa bent over her little sister, smoothing back the tousled hair from the girl's forehead.

Nikki, Carly, Dr. Phyllis, Aunt Marta, and Callan settled themselves in the waiting room. Dr. Phyllis poured herself a cup of coffee from a carafe on a side table, then looked at Nikki and Carly.

"Most of this story has sounded fairly jumbled to me, and there hasn't been a chance to ask questions until now," Dr. Phyllis said. "Why don't the two of you fill me and Marta in on the details of how this happened to Tory?"

Nikki glanced at Carly, waiting for her to begin, but Carly sat silent, as tongue-tied as she'd been that first day when Dr. Phyllis surprised her in the middle of her imitations.

Nikki sighed and began. "Tory and Marissa came by for their kittens just as we were getting ready to go out jogging. Tory said she had always wanted to jog, too—like Carly, of course."

She smiled at Carly, sorry for her outburst back on the path and thinking only that Carly would be flattered by her mention of Tory's obvious hero-worship. But Carly was far from flattered.

"Oh, sure!" she burst out before Nikki could continue.

"Blame it all on me!" She pushed herself up off the brown vinyl couch where she'd been sitting and began pacing the room angrily. "It's *always* me, isn't it?"

"But Carly," Nikki began, "I didn't mean—"

Dr. Phyllis caught Nikki's eye and gave a barely perceptible shake of her head, signaling her to let Carly proceed. But it was unnecessary because Carly went right on without even noticing the interruption.

"How was I supposed to know Tory would knock herself out to keep up with me, anyway? And that she'd stick her foot in a stupid groundhog hole? I didn't mean for any of that to happen. This *isn't* my fault, you know. It isn't!"

"Carly, no one said anything about it being your fault," Aunt Marta said, her voice quiet.

Carly whirled around to stare out the window and crossed her arms over her chest. "No? Well, you may not have *said* it, but that's what you're all thinking!"

Ever since the accident, Nikki had been worrying that the "new" Carly was on her way back, and now she realized with a sinking feeling that it was true. The defensiveness, the belligerence, the defiant look in her eyes were all there again.

Carly swiveled on one foot to face them. "I was just trying to be nice to Tory. I showed her how to do her hair and listened to her talk about a million and one things she wanted to tell me. I didn't make her go jogging. I didn't make her follow me up the hill. I didn't make her do *any* of those things!"

She glared at them angrily, daring them to disagree, but all Nikki could think was how much she looked like a frightened animal backed into a corner.

Callan shifted slightly in his chair. "I don't believe anybody here thinks you *made* her do anything, Carly, not in the way you're saying. But the truth is, all of us could see she was trying to imitate everything you did right from the beginning—"

"Oh, so you're saying it *is* my fault then, Mr. Know-It-All? You always have all the answers for everything, don't you, Callan? You started criticizing me the day I got here, and you haven't stopped since. You're as bad as Nikki, who goes snooping around under my bed trying to find heaven knows what. She always finds something to criticize, too!"

She turned back to Nikki. "You say I shouldn't always want to change things, like doing the makeover and all. But you're the one who *really* wants to change things—you want to change *me!* You don't like the way I exercise, you don't like the way I eat, you don't like the fact that I've been losing weight. Well, I'll tell you what I think, Nikki. I think you're *jealous*, that's what I think!"

Nikki sat red-faced and stunned as Carly stomped off down the hall, then got to her feet to follow. Dr. Phyllis put up a hand to stop her.

"Nikki, let her go. She's obviously feeling very guilty about Tory, and when people can't deal with their guilt, they often turn it on others. Like you. Or Callan. Try to give her a little space. And remember, it's not you."

Not me? Nikki thought. *If you only knew! Carly's absolutely right. I think I've been jealous of her since we were in diapers.*

She walked to the window and stared out, pretending to study the gray sky, but the quiet voice, the same one she'd heard in the car, had her attention again.

Nikki, it's time for you to deal with this issue.

Nikki caught her bottom lip between her front teeth and frowned.

The voice went on. *It's eating you up inside and getting in the way of your relationships.*

For a few seconds, Nikki tried to pretend she didn't recognize the voice. But it was the same voice she'd heard during Evan's adoption ceremony, the one she'd heard in the motel room in California when she had been at her wit's end. It was the same one she sometimes heard when she knelt beside her bed with a Bible open in front of her, asking the Lord to speak. And each time she heard it, she wanted to avoid facing the truth, but the voice gently but firmly persisted until she listened.

Nikki dropped her gaze and stared at the toes of her running shoes, glad her back was to the others.

How could I not be jealous of Carly? She always gets all the attention.

Is it just Carly?

Nikki swallowed and tears welled up in her eyes. *No, not just Carly. I've always compared myself with* all *my friends.*

Nikki thought back over her years in high school. She thought about Lauren and the other girls she hung out with back at Millbrook High in Ohio. She named each one, oblivious to the elevator music piped in over the speakers, or the sporadic paging of doctors' names, or even of the conversation going on behind her between Dr. Phyllis and Aunt Marta and Callan. *I was jealous of them all.*

But why, Nikki? Why? the voice asked.

That's obvious! I wished I could be pretty, or smart, or popular like them!

But what's wrong with being who I made you to be?

She stood absolutely still, listening.

You're like the mockingbird—always trying to sing someone else's song. Don't you know I made you just the way I want you to be, Nikki?

Nikki waited.

Didn't you say you trust Me for eternity, Nikki? the voice urged her gently.

"Yes, Lord," she said, her voice a small and timid whisper.

Then what about trusting Me for right now?

The ludicrousness of it hit her full in the face. She didn't even try to answer. Instead, she muttered something to the others and left in the same direction Carly had gone. She had some idea of finding another lounge, an empty one, and after a few tries, she did.

The weather channel was on, the meteorologist pointing out on the map behind her the hurricane that showed up like a white cotton candy swirl over the Gulf of Mexico. Nikki listened for a minute as the meteorologist with amazingly white teeth and perfectly coifed hair talked about the storm, which she predicted would move back out to sea.

Nikki punched the remote button to turn off the TV and turned to face the empty room. She wished she had enough nerve to get down on her knees—it seemed a more appropriate posture, somehow, for surrender—but instead she dropped onto the nubby blue upholstery of the corner chair, crossed her arms on her knees and leaned her head on her forearms.

You're right, of course, Lord, she began. *It's pretty stupid to say I trust You with my whole eternity and yet refuse to trust You with right now. I guess there could be worse things than my totally unpredictable hair. Than making good grades and looking like it—*

No, Nikki, the voice prodded her. *That won't do. That's* resignation, *and resignation is how you respond when someone's given you a raw deal but you've decided not to complain anyway. It makes you look good, but there's no trust in it.*

Nikki sighed, frustrated, and sent up a plea for help sorting things out in her mind. Then, in an instant, things came clear. She began to pray again. *So, if I've got this right, I've got to trust You enough to accept—no, to* welcome—*whatever You send me. With open arms, right?*

There were no words in her head this time, but in their place, Nikki could have sworn she heard a sigh of relief.

Fifteen

PEACE FILLED NIKKI'S HEART. It was as though a battle had ended, a battle she hadn't even realized she'd been fighting. After a while, she stood up and combed through her hair with wide-spread fingers, using the darkened TV screen as a mirror. Then she turned and started down the hall.

She had to find Carly right away. Tell her it was okay. Tell her she could trust God to help her through whatever it was that was tearing her up inside. That it was safe to be herself.

If Nikki could just put into words what she'd learned, just make her understand, then maybe Carly would go back to normal. *And stay that way.* She glanced up, saw she was across the hall from a rest room, and decided to take a minute to check herself in a real mirror.

She pushed open the heavy wooden door and entered the narrow, two-stall rest room. She started toward the mirror, but sounds from behind the closed door of one stall stopped her dead in her tracks.

They were retching sounds—sounds Nikki remembered

all too well from the first months of her pregnancy with Evan.

Nikki's stomach lurched, and she hesitated a moment, unsure what to do. Again the gagging, retching sound tore through the small room. Somebody was getting really, *really* sick in there.

And I'm going to be just as sick if I don't get out of here. She turned back toward the door quietly, reaching for the door handle, thinking how embarrassed she'd be if someone came in and heard her throwing up in a public rest room.

But just as her hand made contact with the door handle, the toilet flushed and the movement of the person's feet inside the stall drew Nikki's eyes downward toward the shoes. Her eyes widened. The shoes had blue and white laces. Laces with the Chicago Cubs logo woven into them. The chances of anyone besides Carly in a women's rest room in Lima, Virginia, wearing running shoes with those particular laces were slim to none.

The stall door swung open, and Carly's face showed an expression of shock at seeing Nikki there. Her face was pale, and she held on to the metal frame of the door with one hand, but she still managed to go on the attack.

"What are you doing here?" she began, her voice sharp. "Snooping again?"

Nikki's high hopes of talking to Carly fell. There was no way to get through to her when she was this angry. She turned and left before Carly could say another word.

Tory's ankle had a trimalleolar fracture, just as the doctor had feared. When Nikki arrived back in the waiting room, she found the doctor explaining to Aunt Marta, Dr. Phyllis, and Callan that there was a "fracture of the lateral and medial malleoli of the right ankle joint" and a whole lot of other words Nikki didn't catch.

There would be a long wait while the bones were set and the cast put in place, so the four of them went across the street to Burger King for lunch. Carly, who eventually re-emerged from the hospital rest room, opted to stay put. When they got back, Tory, now full of pain medicine, was smiling and joking with everyone, once again enjoying her position as the center of attention as she coaxed all the nurses to sign her pink cast.

The next three days were quiet ones, marked by billowy gray clouds overhead and heavy, sporadic downpours as Hurricane Beatrice stalled in place, unable to make up its mind which way to turn. The air felt thick and soggy, and Nikki finally gave up all efforts to control her frizzy hair. She simply pulled it back in a ponytail and tried not to look in the mirror any more than was necessary.

Marta and Dr. Phyllis were gone most of the time, meeting with musicians Marta needed to interview. When they were home, the two older women took Nikki and Carly and drove to the Barkers' house each day for a short visit with Tory, who was still on pain medication and slept much of the time.

The room Carly and Nikki shared was more like an armed camp than a place to laugh together or share confidences. When they first arrived home from the hospital on Monday afternoon, Nikki had gathered all her courage and tried again to talk to Carly.

"Carly," she'd said, making her voice as gentle and non-confrontational as possible, "I don't understand everything that's going on with you. I thought at first it was just this guy, Jeremy. But now I think maybe you need some help with—"

That was as far as she'd gotten before Carly struck back with all the force she could muster. "I don't need *help*,

Nicole, and stop saying it! You, of all people, should be talking! At least *I* didn't get pregnant. If I *did* need help, it wouldn't be from you, okay?"

Nikki's face had burned with shame as she saw herself through Carly's eyes, and the feelings hung like an impenetrable wall between them.

Carly went jogging or walking whenever the rain let up. When the weather kept her inside, she lay on her bed, her head propped up with her hand, doing one quiz after another from her makeover magazine. When Nikki thought back to her earlier idea of having devotions with Carly and praying with her, it seemed like a childish fantasy. Except for an occasional "Excuse me, may I get something out of my dresser drawer?"—said with exaggerated politeness—there was not a word spoken between them. The tension was so thick that the air in the room nearly crackled, and Nikki knew an explosion was building.

But Nikki hated explosions, so she was gone from the room as often as possible, glad that Callan, at least, was always willing to talk. In between practice sessions, he often sprawled on the porch swing, reading or listening to his portable CD player. Whenever Nikki headed toward one of the big wicker rockers that faced the swing, he looked up eagerly, glad to see her. It was during one of their talks that he gave her an unexpected look into his own past, and in doing so handed her a key to helping Carly.

They had been discussing Annie's situation, with Nikki recounting Aunt Marta's indignant words from the previous evening.

"Aunt Marta and Dr. Phyllis were over there again, trying to talk sense into Mr. Slayton," Nikki told him. "Marta said he's talking a whole different story now, but that it's almost worse than before."

Callan shifted a little in the swing where he was sitting,

the wooden slats creaking beneath his weight. "How could it get *worse?*"

"Well, remember how at first he kept saying that he'd never let her go to the university with Dr. Phyllis and my aunt? That they were just after money?"

Callan nodded.

"Now, Aunt Marta says, he just looks at Annie and tells her, 'It's up to you, girl. You know you can do what you want. I'm not going to stand in your way.' "

Callan frowned. "You know, if I didn't know Len Slayton, I'd say that's a great change. Unfortunately, I *do* know him, and that doesn't sound like him at all. He's got something up his sleeve."

"That's what's so awful about it," Nikki answered. "Aunt Marta says it gives her the creeps. He says all the right words, but the whole time he's talking, he's staring at Annie in this weird way. She says Annie looks scared to death, but they don't know what she's scared of. Even Marissa's confused about it. She came over yesterday to see the kittens for just a few minutes—she doesn't seem to want to leave Tory alone for very long these days—and told me the same thing. Marissa says Annie's getting more and more upset, but she won't say why."

Callan shut his eyes and swung back and forth silently for a moment.

Nikki added, "Both my aunt and Dr. Phyllis say it's almost like her father is holding something over her head."

Callan swung back and forth quietly for another minute, then crossed his arms over his chest. "I'll tell you one thing, Nikki, that guy has scared me for a long time. He is really strange."

Nikki remembered the threatening way he'd stared at her and Carly the first day they'd come into town. "Yeah, I know what you mean," she said.

Callan sat up then, changing the subject. "What about you, Nikki? You going to make it through all this?"

"All what?"

"Come on, Nikki. Everybody can see what's going on with Carly," he answered. "I mean, it can't be easy sharing a room with her when she's like this."

"Actually, it's probably easier now than when we first got here," Nikki said with a casual shrug. "She's not hounding me about those dumb quizzes anymore. Anyway, at least we're not arguing—it's pretty hard to fight when you're not even speaking."

Callan gave her a long, level look, and Nikki flushed.

"Okay, okay. You're right," she admitted. "It's not easy." She drew her knees up to her chest and locked her arms around them. "It's like . . . like . . . she's turned into somebody I don't even know." She stopped to listen to the raindrops drumming steadily on the roof, then continued. "Carly is one of my best friends, Callan. We've always been different, but that never seemed to matter before. Not much, anyhow. I mean, just last winter, Carly was one of the ones who helped me through a really, really tough time. She was always praying for me and encouraging me and telling me to listen to the Lord. And now look at her, Callan. *Look* at her! It's like she doesn't care about anything except how she looks. It's like that's become her . . . her *god*, you know?"

Callan nodded gently, his face sad. "I went through that a couple years ago. Not exactly the way Carly is now, but I thought I didn't matter if I didn't look a certain way—" he nodded toward his damaged leg "—or have a perfect body."

"You?" Nikki said in surprise. "What do you mean?"

"You haven't heard the whole story, Nik," he answered. "I told you the other day about my mother, who was too busy to bring me to lessons. I had a dad, too. But when I was diagnosed with muscular dystrophy, he walked out.

Not right away." Callan gave a short, humorless laugh. "He waited around till I was old enough to remember him—about six. By then he'd taken me to every doctor he could find. Then he told my mother he couldn't stand seeing me this way anymore."

Nikki stared at Callan and felt something lurch in her chest. Her mother and father would never win any honors as parents, that was for sure. But leaving a six-year-old because he had a disease, well, even *her* parents wouldn't do that.

"I'm so sorry" was all she could think to say, knowing immediately how inadequate the words sounded.

"Yeah," Callan answered and then fell silent for several seconds before going on. "It was a tough time. When he finally figured out there was nobody who could 'fix' me, he packed up and left. At first, he'd come and visit me, telling me he really loved me and all that. But even a kid understands that you don't leave someone you love. Finally, he just stopped coming altogether."

Nikki hugged her arms tighter around herself. "Oh, Callan . . . "

He looked up and smiled. "It's okay now, Nikki. My dad's rejection was tough, even tougher than coming to terms with the fact that I have a disease that will just keep getting worse and worse. But I found out that God can turn everything in my life to my good, if I let Him. Even having my father dragging me around to all those specialists turned out to be a good thing. I ended up working with an occupational therapist who figured out everything that would get in my way or cause me problems, and she came up with all these exercises to help me function as well as possible."

Nikki frowned. "I know a little about physical therapy because my grandmother had a stroke last year and that's part of her recovery, but I don't think I've ever heard of occupational therapy before."

"Occupational therapy taught me to be as independent as I could so I don't always have to rely on other people. Not that it made having muscular dystrophy all right. For the longest time, I kept trying to change myself, kept trying to be somebody else—somebody my dad could love, I guess. I figured if my own father could walk out and leave me, I must not be worth very much. For a couple years, I *hated* who I was."

Callan shifted forward on the swing seat and continued. "Then I realized I was looking at myself through the wrong set of eyes."

Nikki raised her eyebrows in question. "You just figured all this out by yourself?"

Callan laughed, a real laugh this time. "No, it was Dr. Phyllis who finally turned on the lights for me. I was taking lessons from her back then, too. And every week when I came, I must have been a giant pain in the neck. I wouldn't practice all week, so of course I never knew my music. I'd argue with everything she said. I just wanted to lash out at everybody. But somehow Dr. Phyllis knew what I needed. She just kept making me talk, and she kept listening. The way she was always there for me convinced me I must be worth *something*. And she's told me since that she prayed for me every day."

"How long were you like that?" Nikki asked.

"About two years," Callan answered. He said something more, but another sudden downpour drowned out his words. They waited through the pounding of the rain, and when it died down, Nikki asked, "What'd you say? That last thing?"

"Dr. Phyllis told me she knew that when I was pushing her away the hardest, that's when I needed her most."

The rain came down harder throughout the afternoon and early evening. It was no longer sporadic, as it had been earlier, but steady and intense, as though Beatrice had decided to come after them with a vengeance. Wind gusted around the house in sharp bursts that rattled the wooden shutters and made the old structure creak and groan.

As the dim gray light began to fade into evening, Nikki came downstairs from the bedroom to find something to eat. At the bottom of the stairs, she hesitated. Even over the noise of the wind and rain, she could make out sounds coming from the music studio. Although she couldn't decipher the words, someone was obviously very angry. A quieter voice answered, then the angry voice came again. As Nikki got closer, she could tell that it was Carly. The door of the studio slammed shut, and Carly stomped down the hall. She brushed past Nikki without a word and disappeared in the direction of the kitchen.

Nikki went to the studio doorway and peeked inside. Callan was sitting on one of the black piano benches, staring at the keys.

"Everything okay?" Nikki asked.

Callan patted his head and face, then grinned a little. "I guess so. She didn't bite my whole head off—just most of it."

Nikki rolled her eyes and smiled back at him.

Later on, Carly and Nikki, still barely speaking to one another, curled up in the two green-cushioned rockers in the family room section of the kitchen, with Callan on the loveseat in between, and switched on the weather channel.

The satellite picture of the hurricane was frightening. Beatrice had moved back out over the Atlantic, picked up momentum, and turned northwest toward the eastern shore of the United States.

The meteorologist, Nikki noticed, was the same woman

she'd watched in the hospital waiting room, with the brilliant white teeth and perfect hair. This time, however, the woman had a worried look around her eyes and her words came with more urgency.

"People along the Outer Banks should stay tuned to check evacuation plans for their local area. The coast guard is urging all beachfront homeowners to take valuables with them if at all possible and to vacate immediately—"

"Wow," Callan said, shaking his head. "Some storm! We're a couple hundred miles inland, and we're still going to get pounded." He pushed himself up and reached for his crutches. "I'd better go call my mom and make sure she's okay."

"I hope Aunt Marta and Dr. Phyllis can get home tonight," Nikki said. "The interview they had this morning was east of here, wasn't it? That means they're probably getting it worse than we are."

They switched to the local newscast, and Callan waited to watch the latest update with them, listening to reports of one accident after another caused by the heavy downpours. The lead story was about the semi truck that had slammed into the side of the Lima bridge while trying to avoid hitting two cars involved in a minor fender bender just ahead of it.

The lights flickered low for a second, then brightened back up, and Carly breathed an audible sigh of relief. Nikki remembered how much Carly had always hated the dark.

There was another roof-rattling gust of wind, and raindrops pounded like tiny bullets against the windowpanes. The noise was so loud that for a moment none of them realized the phone was ringing, then Nikki jumped up to answer it.

"Hello?" she said into the receiver.

The voice on the other end sounded far away, distorted. "Dr. Phyllis? Is that you?"

"I'm sorry, Dr. Phyllis is gone until late tonight. This is Nikki Sheridan. I'm a friend who's staying with her."

"Oh, Nikki." The voice sounded both frustrated and perplexed. "This is Lou Barker—Tory and Marissa's mom."

Nikki listened while the older woman told her how she had gone along with her husband on his bread route that afternoon so he could drop her off at a store in Lima.

"We thought we'd only be gone an hour or two," she explained. "I had to get groceries, and I knew Tory would be all right with Marissa for that long. You know she can't get around so easy with that big cast on, and sometimes her ankle still pains her so much. . . . Anyway, Yarnell said we'd be home by supper at the latest, so I came along. But Nikki . . . you still there, hon?"

"I'm here," Nikki answered.

"Well, the bridge is closed. There was this accident—I don't know if you saw the news—"

"About that truck? Yes, we just saw it."

"Well, that's the only way we can get home from Lima, over that bridge. And I don't have any idea how long it'll be till they can get it open again. So I was hoping Dr. Phyllis could go over to our house to be with the girls until we get home."

"Aunt Marta said they'd be late, and now, with the way the weather is, it could take them even longer."

There was a hesitation on the other end of the line before Mrs. Barker spoke again. "I hate to ask, but . . . could we bother you and Carly . . . to maybe go and sit with the girls till we get home? Do you have a car there?"

"Sure, we have Aunt Marta's car. They took Dr. Phyllis's car this morning," Nikki said.

"The girls would be so relieved to have you there. And it'd sure put our minds at ease. You could just take your night things and sleep in our bed, because I don't know exactly when we'll be able to get home."

Nikki knew exactly what she had to say, but she stalled for a moment. The thought of being stuck with Carly—in the car and at the Barkers'—made her squirm.

"Well, sure, we'll be glad to," she finally answered.

Sixteen

CARLY SHOWED LITTLE EMOTION when Nikki told her where they were going. She got up and left the family room, saying only, "I'll go get my stuff."

Once her footsteps died away down the hall, Nikki glanced at Callan where he still stood by the couch. "Will you be okay here?" she asked, then saw immediately it had been the wrong thing to say.

Callan put on a face that made Nikki laugh. "Oh, I figure I can probably muddle along till you women get back." Then his eyes turned serious. "I'll be praying, Nikki. I hope you and Carly can work some things out."

Nikki shook her head as she walked toward the hall. "I don't know, Callan. I think she's decided to shut everyone out. I can't see her changing right now."

She was just about to walk through the doorway when he called quietly after her.

"Don't give up on her, Nikki. Remember, when she's pushing you away the hardest, that's when she needs you most."

Nikki's eyes filled with tears, and she blinked hard, then

nodded before she turned toward the stairs.

Nikki drove the two miles to the Barkers' cautiously, leaning over the steering wheel and squinting, trying to see the road ahead in each brief instant after the wipers scraped the window bare of streaming water.

There was no conversation between her and Carly. *Unless you count me saying, "Don't let me miss the turnoff, okay?"* Nikki thought, her lips pressed tight together in frustration.

Carly didn't even acknowledge her question, but when they came to the turnoff, she pointed her index finger to the right, toward the Barkers' long, unpaved driveway.

Nikki hesitated, looking at the drive streaming with mud, then turned the Taurus cautiously toward the house. Inwardly, she was fuming. Words she'd like to hurl in frustration at Carly tumbled over one another in her mind, pushing and shoving to get out, but just when she thought she could stand it no longer and opened her mouth, Callan's words echoed in her head.

"When she's pushing you away the hardest, that's when she needs you most."

Right, Nikki thought. She pushed away some angry thoughts and closed her mouth, then pulled the car up as close to the Barker house as possible, trying to avoid running through as much of the drenching rain as possible. *But if that's the case, I'll need You to give me wisdom, Lord, because I haven't got a clue what to do here.*

Nikki grabbed her overnight case from the backseat and tried to sound funny. "Are you ready to move *fast*, lady?" She peered at the house through the space cleared by the windshield wipers and noted with a sinking feeling that the windows were completely dark.

Carly reached across the seat and honked the horn three times. "Maybe if we let her know we're here, Marissa will meet us at the door, so we won't get so soaked standing there," Carly said.

They dashed to the front door and, sure enough, by the time they got up the steps, Marissa was waiting behind the open door, a flashlight in her hand. Nikki and Carly ducked inside the house, dripping wet.

Marissa's voice was a combination of relief and worry. "I am *so* glad to see you guys! I thought at first you were Mom and Dad, but when I heard the horn, I knew it wasn't them."

"Didn't your mother call and tell you we were coming?" Nikki asked.

Marissa shook her head. "The lights and phone went out a little while ago."

"Marissa? Marissa, where are you? Who's out there with you?" Tory's voice, normally so confident, quavered a little as it floated out of the darkness from the direction of the living room.

Marissa turned immediately, gesturing with the flashlight for them to follow her. "It's Carly, Tory. And Nikki. We're coming right now."

Carly started for the living room, and Nikki set her bag on the floor next to Carly's, then pushed them both up against the wall so no one would trip over them in the darkness.

"Marissa!" Tory called again.

"Coming!" Marissa answered. "She doesn't like me to leave her for very long these days," she told Nikki.

Nikki followed her, thinking with amazement that Tory's accident may have been the best thing that ever happened to the sisters' relationship.

When they walked into the living room, Tory gave a sigh of relief. "That's better. I could hardly see in here without that flashlight."

Carly went to one of the recliners, and Marissa sat down on the floor in front of the couch where Tory lay. But Nikki stood nervously, listening to the steady roar of rain on the shingled roof. She knew from the forecast on the weather channel that the storm was supposed to grow even worse in the next several hours, and that meant the power would almost surely be off all night. What if one of the huge trees over the house came down in the wind? What were they supposed to do about fixing dinner?

As she stood in the doorway worrying, Nikki noted anxiously that Marissa's flashlight dimmed suddenly, came back to full power, then dimmed again.

Tory drew in her breath with a little gasp. "Nikki, what'll we do if the batteries go out?"

Now that's what we need here, Nikki thought. *Another problem.* She glanced at Carly, stretched out on one of the recliners, her feet up on the extended footrest, and felt a stab of anger. Ever since they got here a week ago, it had been Carly this and Carly that and isn't Carly great. But now that there was trouble, everyone expected Nikki to have all the answers. Carly seemed hardly aware that there was a problem. *Even Tory can see that Carly's no help like this, looking kind of pathetic, off in some little world of her own, the same way she's been ever since the accident.*

The flashlight dimmed again, and Marissa's face creased with worry. "I don't think we have any more batteries in the house, Nikki. I checked the flashlight my parents keep by their bed, but that one doesn't work at all."

"That's okay," Nikki said as calmly as she could. "We'll find candles. Your mother has some candles, doesn't she?"

Marissa and Tory looked at each other, then back at Nikki. "Just the big one there on the end table," Tory said. Marissa flashed her light across the fat, cream-colored candle in an ornate brass holder so Nikki could see it. "But

Mom would never let us burn that—Aunt Barb gave it to her when I was really little, and she's never even lit it," Tory said uncertainly.

"Believe me, she'll understand," Nikki answered. "We have to have *some* light. So where are the matches?"

As Marissa and Nikki headed into the kitchen with the flashlight, Nikki said, "Carly, why don't you keep Tory company while we go find the matches?"

"Okay," Carly said.

Nikki turned and followed Marissa to the kitchen, a funny ache growing in her chest about Carly. *But I'll have to worry about her later*, she thought, pushing it aside. *Right now I have to take care of Tory and Marissa.*

By the time they found the matches and lit the candle and two small oil lamps that Marissa found in her parents' bedroom, the room seemed almost cozy. The wind lashed the rain against the windows, and the air grew chilly with the dampness. Nikki shivered, glad she'd changed from shorts to jeans before they left Dr. Brummels's house.

There was leftover pizza in the refrigerator and, since the kitchen oven was electric, Nikki doled the pizza out to everyone cold. They were one piece short, and Nikki was surprised to hear Marissa offer to give up hers for Tory. Instead, Carly insisted she wasn't hungry at all and refused to eat a slice. Nikki searched the pantry by flashlight and found a half a bag of chips. Carly just looked at Nikki when she held the bag out to her, then shook her head and turned away. When everyone finished, Nikki threw away the paper plates and napkins, then they sat looking at one another.

No TV, no CDs. What now? Nikki wracked her brain, trying to come up with something fun that required no electricity and almost no light. *This could be a very long evening.*

"I know what we could do!" Nikki said, turning to Carly. "Which quiz are you on, Carly? We could all take it together.

You brought your magazine, didn't you?"

Carly sat still on the recliner. She barely nodded, show- ing no excitement. "Yeah, it's in my bag."

"Well, go get it!" Nikki said, working hard at livening things up.

Carly shook her head back and forth. "I don't feel like doing the quizzes anymore."

She folded her arms across her chest. In the soft light of the oil lamps, Nikki could see her hair still had its golden sheen, but her face was tight and drawn. Nikki's heart ached for her, watching Carly insist on trying to make her own way through trouble too big for her to handle alone.

But Lord, I don't know how to reach her. I've tried everything I can think of and she doesn't even hear me. How am I supposed to get through to her?

Even over the din of the driving rain against the roof and windows, it was as though Nikki heard God answer her clearly in her heart.

You're not supposed to—I am.

She sat perfectly still, waiting for something more as the conversation between Tory and Marissa went on around her. Finally, she gave up and breathed a sigh, feeling let down, then jerked upright to a sudden pounding at the door.

Marissa grabbed the flashlight, and both she and Nikki hurried to see who was there. It was Annie, soaked and dripping, trying to talk but unable to get words out between hiccups and the shivers.

In a matter of minutes, they'd sent her to the bathroom with dry towels and a set of Marissa's clothes to change into. When Annie emerged a few minutes later, Marissa's too-big jeans were gathered around her waist with a belt.

"I put my horse in the barn with yours and rubbed him down real good, Marissa," she explained.

"You rode Renegade in this rain?" Marissa asked.

"I couldn't help it." Annie's voice shook. "I had to get away from my dad. I just couldn't stand it anymore."

Marissa turned and looked at Nikki, a plea for help in her eyes, and Nikki struggled to remember how grown-up a 17-year-old could seem in the eyes of a 13-year-old.

Nikki spoke as gently as she could to Annie. "Can you tell me about it, Annie? I don't know if I can help, but I'll try."

Annie stared at her for a long moment, then nodded her head up and down.

"Are you guys *ever* coming back in here?" Tory called. "It's not fair that I don't know what's going on just 'cause I can't get around!"

Marissa shrugged apologetically. "It won't make any difference, as long as Annie doesn't mind talking in front of Carly—Tory's heard most of what's going on, anyway. At least she'll stop bugging us that way."

They moved back into the living room and waited while Annie settled herself in one of the recliners, cleared her throat a few times, then carefully unfolded the limp tissue in her hand and blew her nose. She wadded the tissue back up and then finally began talking, light from the oil lamps flickering across her thin face.

"My dad—he drinks a lot," she said. "He didn't always drink so much, I don't think, but I do remember my mom telling him not to. After she died when I was eight, he said there was nothing else for him to do at night and that a couple beers helped him not feel so bad. But it got to be a lot more than a couple, and then he lost his job at the mill. He's been mad about it ever since. He logs up on the mountain by himself, but he doesn't like it. So now he drinks more, and when he does, he gets madder than ever."

She stopped to blow her nose again, and Nikki pushed

the box of tissues on the coffee table toward her.

"What happens then, Annie?" Nikki asked. "When he gets madder than ever?"

Annie took a long time answering, folding and refolding the tissue. At last she put it in the pocket of Marissa's jeans and looked at the wall behind Nikki.

"He sometimes takes off in his truck," she said in a voice so soft that Nikki had to lean forward to hear over the drumming of the rain outside. "I don't know where he goes. Well, most of the time I don't."

"But sometimes you do?" Nikki asked.

Annie sat still.

"Annie?" Nikki coaxed, wishing desperately that an adult would suddenly materialize in the room to get the younger girl through this.

"Once I did. Last year." Her voice dropped even more. "He was still drunk when he came home, and he kept talking and talking about what happened. There was an accident—"

She broke off and looked around at them all.

There was no sound but the rain hitting the windows like tiny bullets.

"People got hurt. Real bad." Annie said the words as though they were too heavy to keep inside any longer. "The one lady's still in a coma. . . ."

Marissa cracked all her knuckles at once, then looked up, startled, and whispered, "Oops, sorry," to no one in particular. Tory stopped chewing her gum and sat perfectly quiet.

Suddenly, Callan's account of the accident at the stop sign in Wald's Ford flashed through Nikki's mind. He had said the driver, a guy who drank a lot, hadn't been tested in time to prove whether or not he was drunk. That he got off on some kind of technicality. She remembered all those bouquets in the chain-link fence and thought of her aunt's description of the flower bed Annie was so proud of.

"Somebody's putting them there in memory of the accident," Callan had said. *"Or to say they're sorry."*

"You never told anybody, did you, Annie?" Nikki asked.

Annie shook her head back and forth in slow motion.

"You just kept putting flowers there, didn't you?"

This time Annie's head moved up and down, still in slow motion.

"Why didn't you tell anyone?"

"He said it was my fault. He used to say that if I behaved better, if I wouldn't argue with him about my singing, he wouldn't get drunk."

"What does he say now?"

"He says if I ever tell *anybody* he was drinking before he left the house that night, he'll tell the whole county it was my fault."

"Your fault! Why?" Nikki burst out.

Annie looked away. "Because I made him so mad that night we had a big fight." She hung her head. "I kept reminding him how Mom always told him not to drink so much. And that I didn't want to sing the way he wants me to. He says I have to put on all this stupid makeup and act sexy and—"

Nikki stopped her. "I know, Annie. We heard him say those things that first night you sang at the festival."

Annie put her face in her hands and said, "He says if people find out the truth, they'll sue us for everything we own and take away our house and truck and put him in jail, and I'll be all alone. But I don't want to keep his secret anymore. I don't want him holding it over my head, and I don't want him yelling at me like he was tonight. I really need help." Then she looked up and held out her hands in a pleading gesture. "This is the biggest problem I've ever had, and I don't know what to do about it."

Nikki listened to the rain, wondering frantically what to say. Then she remembered what she'd already learned. This was God's problem to solve, not hers.

Okay, Lord, she prayed quickly, *I'm handing this over to You. Please show me how to help Annie. And please, Lord, in the middle of all this with Annie, don't forget how much Carly needs help, too.*

❦ *Seventeen* ❧

NIKKI SAT ON THE EDGE of the coffee table in front of Annie, her knees almost touching the younger girl's.

"Annie," she said in the most reassuring tone she could muster, "I'm not a counselor, so I don't know exactly what to say. . . ." She saw Annie's mouth droop with disappointment, and she hurried on. "*But* I can help you find out who to talk to. The most important thing you said was that you need help. That takes a lot of courage—and it's the first step to getting out of this mess."

Nikki's gaze was fixed on Annie's face, but out of the corner of her eye, she noticed something going on in the other recliner. Carly, who had been almost totally withdrawn to this point, was leaning slightly forward toward Nikki and Annie, listening intently.

Nikki didn't want to let on that she noticed Carly's sudden interest in their conversation. Instead, she said, "In fact, admitting you need help is the first step to getting out of *any* mess." *Lord, help me say the right thing,* she prayed.

"I guess we all end up facing problems that are too big to handle alone," Nikki continued. "Nobody gets through life without help. Believe me, Annie, I know." *Believe me, Carly, I know!* "I don't know the answer to your problem, but for now, you're safe here. As soon as the storm lets up and Mr. and Mrs. Barker get here to take care of Tory, we'll take you to Dr. Phyllis and my aunt."

Annie looked at her with a serious expression, then asked in a whisper, "You promise?"

Nikki reached out and squeezed her hands. "I promise."

Annie sat back with a relieved look on her face, and Nikki tried to think what they could do to break the tension in the room.

After some small talk, Tory stretched and started popping her bubble gum again. "Well, we can't watch TV. We can't even play Monopoly, because all we have are these old oil lamps and my mom's candle, and we can't waste them playing games all night. So what now? We sit around here all night with nothing to do?"

Lord, help me think of something to keep the girls busy. Something that'll lighten things up, too. The idea came to her almost at once. "I know what we can do!" Nikki said, sitting up straight in her chair. "Do you have an umbrella, Marissa?"

The girls looked at Nikki as though she were out of her mind.

"You're going out in *this*?" Tory asked, incredulous.

"Just to get something out of the car," Nikki answered.

Within two minutes, she was back inside the house, shaking water off herself and pulling Aunt Marta's tape recorder out from under her shirt, where she'd hidden it to protect it from the downpour.

"Are you gonna make Annie sing into that?" Tory asked.

"I don't have my guitar—" Annie began, but Nikki shook her head.

"No! We're going to play this game I just remembered— one I learned at camp when I was about your age." She cleared a spot on the coffee table among Tory's water bottle and bubble gum wrappers, the fingernail polish remover and red-stained cotton balls, and positioned the recorder in the middle.

"Okay, this is what you do," she started. "Somebody starts a story—with just a few lines—and then stops right in the middle, at an exciting part. Then the next person has to keep going, adding a couple more lines. Then *she* stops, and the next person goes. Get it? And at the end, you have this really, really crazy story, and we all get to listen to it."

She looked around the dim room in the flickering light. Tory's mouth was nearly covered by a rubbery pink bubble that was growing larger by the second.

"Well?" Nikki asked.

The bubble popped with a loud crack. "I think it sounds kind of dumb, if you don't mind my saying so."

Nikki sighed and threw out her hands in frustration. "Fine, Tory. Then *you* think of something to do."

"We could at least try," Marissa said, backing her up loyally. "It's not gonna hurt you or anything, Tory."

Annie nodded her agreement.

Tory glanced across the coffee table at Carly. "I will if Carly does."

Carly glanced up but didn't reply.

"Please, Carly?" Tory begged.

Carly shrugged and nodded. "I guess so. Just don't expect much."

Nikki told Annie and Marissa to sit on the floor, across the coffee table from her. Tory, on the couch behind them, turned on her side to face the recorder.

Nikki waited for Carly to move, then finally said, "Carly, it would help if you'd get closer, okay? The recorder will pick up your voice better that way."

Carly crossed the room and sat on the arm of the couch behind Tory's head.

"Who wants to start?" Nikki asked.

The younger girls were warming up to the idea now, and Tory giggled.

"I know! Here, let me start." She cleared her throat and began, "It was a dark and stormy night—"

They all groaned. "Try not to be so original, would you?" Annie chided.

Their first few tries at creating a story were disasters. Three times, Nikki hit the rewind button to back up the tape and start over. Tory and Marissa were nearly hysterical with laughter now, each try at a story sounding funnier and funnier to them. Even Annie was beginning to laugh a little.

But Carly, still perched on the arm of the couch, one elbow resting on the back and her head propped up by her hand, hadn't said a word. She was listening, Nikki knew, because sometimes she smiled a little at the girls' antics, but she hadn't entered in at all yet.

On the fourth try, Tory took over. "Okay, you guys. Admit it, our own stories are *awful.* Try this one with me." She reached over and switched on the tape recorder and her voice took on a singsong quality. "Once upon a time, there was a little girl named Red Riding Hood."

Marissa put her head in her hands and groaned, and Annie rolled her eyes.

But Tory hushed them with her hand, patting the air in front of her, saying, "Shhh! Just try this one—you be the grandmother, Marissa, and Annie, you be the wolf." She looked up at Nikki. "And you can be that guy—what was he called?"

"The woodcutter!" both Annie and Marissa chimed in.

"Yeah, that's right. You be him, Nikki. Carly, you be Little Red Riding Hood and I'll be the . . . the what do you call it? You know—the one who tells the story."

Carly shook her head. "I think I'll sit this one out, if you don't mind."

Tory began again. "Okay, have it your way. I'll be Little Red Riding Hood, too. Now where was I? There was this girl named Little Red Riding Hood."

Nikki had to marvel at Tory's natural storytelling ability. She told the story as much with her hands as with her words and kept mixing in parts from other fairy tales by mistake. But even so, she ad-libbed so well that she soon had her sister and Annie howling with laughter. Even Nikki laughed so hard that she ended up wiping her eyes.

"So Little Red Riding Hood set off into the woods, her basket under her arm," Tory went on. "And she met a bear— a great, big, giant daddy bear, and he said—"

"*That's* not in this story!" Marissa burst out.

"It's in *my* version," Tory hissed. "Now *hush!*" Then, in a deep, gravelly voice, she went on. " 'You shouldn't be walking through these woods alone, little girl. I'll come with you and keep you safe.' But Little Red Riding Hood said—" and her voice switched to a high-pitched, little-girl timbre " '—No, thank you. I don't need any help.' And she kept on walking. Then Little Red Riding Hood met a . . . a . . . " She paused, her eyes squeezed shut as she thought. "She met a billy goat! A big, gruff billy goat!"

Marissa shook her head, laughing helplessly.

But Tory pressed on. "And the billy goat said, 'Say, little girl, don't you want my help walking through these big, dark woods?' But Little Red Riding Hood said, 'I will do this on my own, thank you very much! I don't need anybody's help. Not anybody's, anybody's, anybody's!' "

Tory cocked her elbow and put one hand on her hip as she said the words, and Nikki couldn't help thinking that the girl sounded exactly like Miss Piggy in the old Muppets movies. Soon, Annie and Marissa were chiming in with characters of their own, each vying for the funniest voice, the craziest line. Finally, Little Red Riding Hood reached the grandmother's house, found the wolf dressed up in bed, and went through the "what big eyes you have" and "what big ears you have" part of the repertoire.

Tory tried to take back control of her story. "And then Little Red Riding Hood said, 'And what big *teeth* you have, Grandmother!' And the wolf said, 'The better to eat you with, my dear' and jumped out of bed and grabbed her. Just then, the woodcutter, who heard her screaming, burst in the door and said—"

She motioned to Nikki, who was supposed to do the woodcutter's part, but Nikki was laughing so hard that all she could think of was, "Are you *sure* you don't need anybody's help?"

And then Carly spoke, startling Nikki, because she hadn't said a word throughout the entire silly story. Her voice was low, barely audible over the rain and wind, but she looked right at Nikki as she spoke.

"I guess I will be Little Red Riding Hood, after all. At this point, I think she'd say, 'You were right all along. I *do* need help.' "

"Hey!" Tory said. "You said you wanted to sit this one out, Carly! Besides, *that's* not in my story!"

Nikki, who had stopped laughing abruptly, hushed her softly, her words barely above a whisper. "It is in this version, Tory."

Carly went on, her brown eyes locked on Nikki's blue ones. "I think she'd say, 'I need lots of help because I can't fight a monster like this alone. I thought I could, but I was wrong.' "

Nikki could see her friend's eyes brim over with tears as she spoke.

Tory was indignant. "Stop it, Carly! You're making her sound like a wimp. Now in *my* version, Little Red Riding Hood . . ."

But Nikki never heard what Tory's Little Red Riding Hood did. Instead, she got up, glad for the darkness that covered the tears trickling down her cheeks, and moved around the coffee table to Carly. The younger girls were so engrossed in their story, each fighting for her turn at the microphone, that they didn't even notice. Nikki put both arms around Carly and hugged her hard, then stepped back to listen as Carly whispered, "I'm sorry, Nik. I've been a total idiot about this whole thing, trying to hide it like this. You were right all along. I need help."

Nikki thought she'd never heard three more beautiful words. She sniffed and wiped her eyes and smiled at her friend. "As soon as the phone's back on, or we get back to Dr. Brummels's, we can talk to Aunt Marta, okay?"

Carly nodded and smiled back, and Nikki knew that, even though there would be battles ahead, her friend was back. For good.

Eighteen

BY MORNING, THE FIERCE RAIN had played itself out. A few gray clouds still scudded across the morning sky, but they were the kind that would burn off with the sun. And all of this, Nikki learned when the electricity came back on and they could get the news, was because temperamental Hurricane Beatrice, contrary to all expectations, had changed her mind yet again and turned eastward toward the open Atlantic.

Annie and Marissa were still sound asleep in the twin beds in the girls' bedroom. Tory was sprawled on her back on the couch with her pink cast propped up on the sofa pillows, mouth open, snoring lightly. Nikki checked on her and grinned. But her smile faded when she returned to the Barkers' master bedroom for her clothes and found Carly gone.

Oh, Lord, not again! Surely she's not out jogging again. Not after everything that happened last night.

She hurried to the front door and opened it.

The mockingbirds were singing in full force, celebrating the end of the storm. But far more important, and more like music to her ears, was the sight of Carly sitting on the top step, her hands linked around her knees, an open Bible on her lap.

Nikki sighed with relief, stepped outside, and pulled the door shut behind her quietly to allow the younger girls to sleep. She sat down on the step beside Carly and smiled at her.

"Good morning."

Carly looked up, and it was obvious from her red eyes that she'd been crying.

"Hi, Nik."

"You okay?"

Carly shrugged a little. "It's harder than I thought, you know?"

Nikki shook her head back and forth. "What's harder?"

Carly reached down and brushed away a blob of mud from the toe of one sneaker. "Not jogging."

"Oh, yeah? My problem is usually just the opposite—*making* myself jog. Maybe you could share some of your love for it with me!"

Carly gave what started out as a grin but ended as more of a grimace. "You don't understand, Nik. It has nothing to do with love. *Nothing.*"

Nikki dropped her teasing tone. "I thought that's why you were out there every morning for an hour—because you loved it so much."

"Try guilt."

"Guilt? What do you mean?" Nikki asked.

"That's why I went running the morning after I promised you I'd cut back on exercise, Nikki. I *had* to." Carly saw the confusion on Nikki's face and tried to explain. "I ate too much the night before, so I *had* to go running. That's what I have to do when I eat too much. I have to . . . get rid of it, you know?"

Nikki's face still registered confusion, and Carly grew frustrated.

"You don't have a clue what I'm talking about, do you? You really didn't know why I was always in the rest room after we ate, did you?"

"Well, after I heard you in the hospital bathroom—"

"I was throwing up, Nikki. Getting rid of everything I ate. *Making myself vomit, Nikki!*"

"Carly, you don't have to—"

"No," Carly said, her voice a mixture of pain and determination. "Let me get it all out on the table, would you? I can't keep up this . . . this balancing act anymore." She looked away and seemed to talk more easily when she stared across the yard at the beginning of the path. "You don't know the half of it, Nik. You don't know about the laxatives. Did you know you can stuff yourself full of just about every junk food you can imagine and still not gain weight? As long as you take enough laxatives, that is." Her voice shook a little. "Of course, you don't feel so hot later on. But, hey, you don't gain any weight."

When Nikki didn't say anything, Carly went on.

"And if you can't stop eating—" she shrugged helplessly "—what else can you do? You've gotta keep the fat off somehow, because being fat is like the absolute worst thing that can happen, right? So you purge—that's the puking part—and then you feel so lousy that you wish you could die. That's what happened when we left here the other day. I threw up in the Barkers' bathroom and was feeling kind of weak. Then my heart started doing all this weird stuff. I was so scared, Nikki. I thought I was gonna die right there on the path. That's when I started to think that maybe, just maybe, this thing might be bigger than I could handle. A friend back in Illinois told me her heart started doing strange stuff after she'd been purging for a couple months, but I never believed it would happen to me. I was really shocked."

Carly's brown eyes filled with tears. She reached out as though to touch Nikki's arm, then drew back, looking ashamed. "I'm sorry, Nikki. I've been really rotten to you this whole trip. I don't know how to explain it, except to say I was so busy trying to hide from myself what was really going on that every time you mentioned anything about it, I got really scared you were figuring things out. I didn't want to face it, you know? So it was easier to blow up at you for 'criticizing' me than to think about what was really going on."

"I didn't even know what *was* going on for a while," Nikki said.

"You didn't?"

"Not at first. I didn't have a clue how wrong things were till I found all that junk food under your bed. I thought you were just moody from PMS or something. I mean, how would I know, Carly? Why would I think losing weight would be this huge deal to you? Look at you, you're gorgeous."

Carly sighed. "But that's not how *I* feel when I look at myself in the mirror. It's—" She stopped and thought for a moment. "I don't how to explain it, except that I've been a real jerk. I—"

"No, you haven't!" Nikki said loyally, but Carly held up a hand to stop her.

"Let me finish, okay? There's some stuff I need to tell you while I can. You know how I kept making fun of you— about you never wanting to change? Nik, you don't know how much I wish sometimes I could be like you. You don't always have to try every single new thing that comes along. It's like you're ... *comfortable* being who you are. And I never have been."

Oh, brother, Nikki thought, waiting for the momentary confusion in her brain to clear. *If only you knew!* But for Carly's sake, she tried to make her answer light. "Let me get this straight. What you're saying now is that being a stick-in-the-mud might have some benefits?"

Carly sniffed and laughed at the same time, wiping her eyes with the back of her hand. "Yeah. Only I couldn't see it. The only thing I could see was that I had to keep up with every new hairstyle, every new type of makeup, everything I saw on TV or in magazines—or nobody would think I mattered." She looked into Nikki's eyes. "Nikki, I'm so tired of trying to do that. I feel like a hamster running frantically on an exercise wheel, getting nowhere. I want to get off."

"Oh, Carly. I know we can get you help," Nikki said emphatically.

"Yeah, I know. I just didn't want it before. I couldn't admit I needed it. I had to be so . . . in control all the time. And the only thing I could really control was the food I ate. But in the end, I couldn't even do that. It started controlling *me*. I had to keep getting on that scale every single day. I *had* to make sure I hadn't gained any weight. Then I'd hear myself lying to you, pretending I was being nice to Tory—" Carly's voice broke, and she put her head in her hands. "And look what I did to her in the end anyway."

"You mean about her ankle?"

"Yeah, that's part of it. Right from the beginning, she wanted to do everything I did. It made me feel important, like I must be right if someone wanted to imitate me. Pretty stupid, huh? But remember that first day we came over here and she didn't want to eat just because I didn't? That killed me. All of a sudden, I saw how you can do bad things to other people even when you don't mean to, just because you're making bad choices yourself.

"And then I felt guilty for eating just so she'd eat—it was

like I was betraying myself—and I had to make sure to throw it all up before we left, before even one little calorie could get into my system. I'd been telling myself I could stop this anytime I wanted. But when you walked in and caught me with the chips, I knew I was just fooling myself. And then when Tory broke her ankle because she was trying to copy me, I fell apart inside. I'm sorry, Nik."

"Don't say you're sorry anymore," Nikki told her. "It's all right. We just have to figure out how to get you help. Your parents must know all the places that deal with eating disorders, don't they?"

Carly wrapped her arms around her knees and hugged them to her chest, staring off toward the path as a mockingbird sang nearby.

"Well, don't they?" Nikki asked again.

"Nikki, my parents know everything," she answered quietly.

"What?" Nikki asked, thinking Carly was trying to be funny.

"They do. Look at them, Nik. Any problem you ever have, they can solve it. Any information you need, they've got it. Anything I try to think through, they've already done it. They love us kids to death. They almost never lose their tempers, and when they do, they come to us and apologize."

This is a problem? Nikki thought. *I think I could handle having parents who are this kind of problem.*

"But I feel like I have to be as good as they are to fit in. Jeff does fine—he always seems to have it together. Abby and Adam aren't old enough to care yet. Then there's me. It's like we have this perfect little family, but on the inside, Nikki, *I don't fit.* I'm all messed up. I have a million questions I can never ask because they aren't the right kinds of questions, you know? And doubts. I can't let my parents know something's this wrong with me. Do you know what that would *do* to them? My dad's a respected doctor—it would hurt his reputation if people knew about my problem."

Nikki bit her lip, wondering if she dared to say what she knew to be true. She decided to soften her words. "I don't think you're giving them a fair chance, Carly. I think they love you enough to help you through anything."

Carly sighed, thinking, then glanced at her. "You do?"

Nikki looked straight into her eyes, trying to pass on her own certainty. "I'd bet my life on it."

Carly didn't answer, but some of the tension lifted from her face.

Nikki started to get to her feet, but Carly motioned her to stop. "I know we have to get Annie over to Dr. Phyllis's and all, but there's one more thing I have to say. Actually, there're two." Twin spots of color appeared over her high cheekbones, and Nikki sensed how hard it was for her to speak. "I've been really rotten to Callan, and you asked me why. I don't know if I can explain it very well, but Callan made me furious. He's crippled, Nikki. Crippled, on crutches, and going to die from what he's got someday. And he's *okay* with it. Can you believe that? You don't have to be around him two minutes before you know Callan's totally comfortable being who he is. I want so badly to be like that, and I can't, and it made me so mad at him. And mad at myself, too, because here I have a ton going for me, and I still can't be happy with who I am." She looked at Nikki. "Do you know what he said to me in the studio yesterday, Nikki?"

Nikki shook her head.

"He said, 'You know what it's like to try to make yourself perfect from the outside in, Carly? It's like putting a new coat of paint on your car before you get it inspected and never worrying about what's going on under the hood.' It made me furious at first, but I thought about that all last night, Nikki. That's what made me really see what I've been doing."

Nikki looked at her with sympathetic eyes.

"And now, the worst thing. . . . You know what I said to you the other night? About not taking help from you because you got pregnant and all?"

Nikki nodded, unable to speak for a moment. The words had burned themselves into her heart.

Tears were coursing down Carly's cheeks in a steady stream now. "I'm *so* sorry, Nikki. I don't even know how to say it. That was absolutely the meanest, rottenest thing I've ever said to anybody."

"It was tough to take, I'll admit it," Nikki answered. "But in a funny kind of way, it helped me. I leaned on you and Jeff and your family and my grandparents to get me through all that—to make me feel that I was okay. But when you said that to me the other night, you left me with no one else to go to but God. So I did. I asked Him again if doing what I did made me . . . worthless. And He reminded me about Moses, who killed a guy, and David, who really messed up *and* killed a guy, and—well, you know all those other people in the Bible better than I do. God forgave them all. And He let them go on and do something with their lives. And I think He will let me, too." She got to her feet. "I think we'd better get the girls up and get over to Dr. Phyllis's. I'm worried Annie's father will come looking for her here."

Nikki reached out her hand to Carly. "Come on. Let me give you a hand."

Carly accepted her help, and the two stood facing one another for a moment. Nikki looked into her friend's brown eyes and smiled.

"It's good to have you back, Carly."

❦ *Nineteen* ❧

EVERYONE WAS ON THE FRONT PORCH, waiting, when Carl and Marlene Allen drove up in the blue rental car two days later. Everyone, that is, except Callan and Carly.

Marta glanced around the porch, then turned to Nikki. "I thought you told Carly her parents were here."

"I did, Aunt Marta, I did. But she and Callan were in the middle of some big conversation in the studio, and all Carly would say was, 'Give us one more minute.'"

"Well, you'd better go let her know her minute is up. I think Carl and Marlene are going to be pretty disappointed if Carly isn't even out here to meet them, after everything they've done to get here this fast."

The screen door behind them opened with a loud squeak as Carly stepped out from the doorway and walked hesitantly toward the blue car that had just braked in the gravel drive. She made her way down the steps and wrapped her arms first around her mother's neck and then her father's.

Nikki swallowed hard as she watched her friend fight to choke back tears.

After long hugs, Carly turned and introduced Dr. Phyllis

to her parents. By this time, Nikki and Marta were in the driveway hugging the Allens, too, and Callan was left standing alone on the porch.

Carly glanced back at him, then motioned for her parents to go up to the porch. "There's somebody else you have to meet." When they got there, Carly said, "This is Callan."

From the way Carly smiled at him as she spoke, Nikki knew their serious conversation in the studio had reaped positive results.

"Callan and I didn't get along at first—" Carly began, then stopped. "I guess that's not really the whole truth. He tried to be friends and I, well, I acted really stupid and treated him badly. He kept saying things that made me think about what I was doing, and I couldn't handle that. But in the end, what he said got through."

Callan shifted his balance uneasily, and Nikki could tell he wanted to turn the conversation away from himself.

"Well, I really am sorry—" Carly began, but Callan broke in.

"Listen, Carly. You already apologized in the studio, and we don't need to go there again because you did it just fine the first time. Let's say it's an old southern custom—to accept a lady's apology."

Over lunch in the sunny kitchen, there was pleasant catch-up conversation, but Nikki could sense an undercurrent of urgency to get to the real problem that had brought the Allens here. They talked about Nikki's grandparents and about Jeff and what the twins were up to back at the lake house in Michigan.

"Jeff's getting ready to leave for U of M next Monday," Marlene said, "so your grandparents are really in charge of the situation, Nikki. You know Abby and Adam think your grandparents are part of our family, too."

"The feeling's mutual," Nikki said, smiling at the thought of how her grandparents' love had always spilled over onto the four Allen children.

Carly set down her iced tea abruptly, unable to hold back her tears.

"What's wrong, honey?" her father asked gently.

She hung her head before she answered. "This is supposed be Jeff's special time—getting ready for college and all. And you had to come here and bail me out instead." She looked up at her parents as tears streamed down both her cheeks. "I really blew it this time."

From her seat beside her daughter, Marlene put a reassuring arm around Carly, and Carl reached across the table and covered her hand with his own.

It seemed a natural moment for Nikki to excuse herself, and Callan did the same. They closed the kitchen door behind them and started quietly toward the front of the house. In the entryway, Callan moved in the direction of the studio, but Nikki stopped him.

"Sounds like you and Carly got everything worked out okay."

Callan nodded, grinning. "Yeah. And I'm glad to report you were right, Nikki. She *can* be as nice as she is pretty. She's just had things mixed up for a little while." He turned toward the studio again. "Listen, I didn't get any practice in this morning because Carly and I were talking, so if you don't mind, I'm going to get to work."

Nikki nodded and pushed open the screen door. She made her way onto the porch and sat on the wooden porch steps, stretching out her bare legs to catch the early afternoon sun. The mockingbird began its recital from the mimosa tree again, and Nikki smiled, remembering.

You're right, Father, she prayed, *I was trying to sing other people's songs, but no more. From now on, I want to work on being*

thankful for who You made me to be—different from every other
person in the world. And thank You for answering my prayers
about Carly so far. Please help them all there in the kitchen. I know
they're deciding the best way to handle the situation. Please—

The soft *clop clop* of horse hooves against the lawn broke
into Nikki's thoughts, and she looked up to see Annie riding
across the lawn.

"Hi, Nikki," she called. She reined in her horse and
stopped in front of the steps, a bouquet of purple asters in
her hands.

"What a gorgeous horse!" Nikki called. "What's his
name, Annie?"

"Renegade," she said.

Nikki ran her hands around the horse's velvety muzzle
and scratched his nose gently, thinking in amazement how
much had happened since the storm ended.

There had been a flurry of activity at Dr. Phyllis's when
Annie returned from the Barkers' with Carly and Nikki.
Once Dr. Phyllis and Marta heard Annie's story, Dr. Phyllis
had called the authorities. Annie's father was taken in for
questioning about the accident the spring before, and the
child welfare department was standing in line to talk to him
next. Meanwhile, at Phyllis's request, Annie was allowed to
stay with her. She had gone home earlier that day to pack
some belongings and make sure the house was locked up.

"Thanks," Annie replied now, glowing with quiet pride
at Nikki's compliment about Renegade. She looped the reins
up over his neck and let him crop the stray grass in the
gravel driveway as she and Nikki sat down on the porch
steps side by side.

"It took you a long time, Annie. You even missed lunch."

Annie shrugged. "Yeah, there was a lot of stuff to do. My
dad left dirty dishes, and I had to get my guitar, and the
flowers had to be watered." She held out the purple flowers

in her arms and asked shyly, "Do you think Dr. Phyllis will like these?"

"She'll love them!" Nikki said. "We'll have to put them in some water so they're still fresh when she gets done talking with Carly and her parents. That was really sweet of you, Annie."

Annie gave a little nod, but her mouth was tense and tight.

"Annie? What's the matter?" Nikki asked gently.

Annie scuffed at the hard-packed dirt in front of the bottom step with the heel of her worn sandal.

"Annie?"

When she spoke, her voice was quiet. "My dad is in jail, Nikki. Because of me."

"But he's being questioned about something *he* did, Annie, not you."

"No. It's because of me. I was the only one who knew. And I told." Her voice was thick with guilt and pain.

Nikki leaned forward intently. "Annie, listen to me. Have you thought what could have happened if you *hadn't* told? That baby's mother is lying in the hospital in a coma because he drove drunk. If someone doesn't stop him, he could hurt someone else. In fact, he could have *killed* someone. You had to tell." Nikki stopped, waiting.

Annie looked up, her face serious. Her eyes searched Nikki's as though looking for answers to questions that were beyond her. Finally, her mouth relaxed from its thin, tight line.

"I know what you're saying is right, Nikki. I think it's just going to take a while for me to feel it inside."

Nikki nodded. "You're going to need someone to talk to about all of this, Annie."

Renegade had polished off the last blades of grass growing up here and there through the gravel and now ambled over to where the girls sat. Annie scratched the space between his ears, then got to her feet.

"I guess I'd better take care of him, Nikki. Dr. Phyllis said I could keep him in one of the empty stalls in her barn." She made a small clucking noise with her tongue, and Renegade followed her obediently as she headed for the barn. Then she stopped and turned back. "I wish you weren't leaving, Nikki. I could talk to you."

She turned away again, and she and Renegade disappeared around the corner of the house.

Nikki waited another half hour, but there was no sign of the discussion in the kitchen ending. She went to the barn and found Annie just finishing with Renegade.

"Annie, would you like to help me with something?" she asked.

"Yeah, sure," the younger girl answered.

"I think this may be a good time to take the kittens over to the Barkers'." She picked up the cardboard pet carrier, which still sat where Marissa had left it the morning of Tory's accident. "Come with me."

Annie's face lit up with one of her rare smiles. "Great idea, Nikki. Tory's about to die from boredom, and I think the kittens would really help keep her busy. C'mon, let's get them."

Within a half hour, Annie and Nikki were parking the Taurus in front of the Barkers' house. The kittens mewed piteously from their cage in the backseat, and Nikki was anxious to get them out of the car and to a place where they would feel safer.

Mrs. Barker looked out the front door to see why McGee and the other hounds had set up such a racket just as Nikki reached into the backseat and brought out the cardboard cage.

"Hi! Oh, you brought the kittens. Tory will be so delighted! And so will we," she added, coming down the front steps to where Nikki and Annie stood. "She's been bugging us constantly to get over to Dr. Phyllis's and get them, but I just wasn't sure this was the time to interrupt, with all you have going on over there. Tory and Marissa are in the back if you'd like to take the kittens out there."

Mrs. Barker turned and put a gentle arm around Annie's shoulders. "Are you doing okay, honey?"

Annie nodded and opened her mouth as though to speak. Then she glanced at Nikki and stopped.

"You know," Nikki said, "I think I'll go ahead and take these kittens around to the girls. You come whenever you're ready, Annie."

Nikki knew that even though Annie had said she could talk to Nikki, she would be leaving in less than a week to go back home. The younger girl needed long-term friends to support her, friends like the Barkers.

By the time Nikki reached the backyard, the kittens were cowering in silence from the motion of the cage and, she supposed, the deep baying of the hounds in the front yard. She tried to put the cage behind her as much as possible so she could surprise the girls. Hidden from the intense heat in the shade of a thick maple tree, Tory was stretched out on a hot-pink plastic and aluminum lounge chair, her bulky cast propped up on pillows. Marissa was on the ground beside her, her head bent over a book she was reading aloud to her sister.

"Hey, you two," Nikki called. "I've got something here for you." She set the cage on the ground beside Marissa, opened the door, and gently pulled out the black and white Boots first, then Patches.

Tory shrieked and reached out both arms for her kitten, laughing as she held it close to her. "Thanks for bringing them, Nikki. I kept asking Mom to go get them, but she didn't want to barge in on Dr. Phyllis with Carly's parents coming and all that's going on with Annie."

The girls were full of questions about Annie and Carly. Nikki did her best to answer, but there wasn't much information she could give.

"Annie's here, inside with your mother, and I think she'll want to tell you herself about what's been going on. As for Carly, her parents flew in from Michigan this morning, and they're over with Dr. Phyllis and Aunt Marta right now, deciding how to help her."

Annie and Mrs. Barker joined them in the backyard then, bringing glasses of lemonade to drink as they watched the kittens' antics. With the Allens at Dr. Phyllis's, Nikki felt she'd better get back before long. Annie begged to stay longer, saying she'd be glad to walk home, so Nikki drove back alone.

Dinner that night was simple—a huge chef salad and iced tea.

"Sorry it's not anything fancy," Dr. Phyllis said.

Marlene Allen laid a gentle hand on the woman's arm and said, "Phyllis, please. After all you've done today, helping us begin to talk through this whole situation with Carly, and putting Carl and me up overnight—please don't apologize for *anything*."

As they sat at the table together, Dr. Phyllis asked Carl Allen to say grace over the food. Nikki shut her eyes at first, but the tiredness in Dr. Allen's voice worried her. She opened her eyes and watched him as he prayed. There were lines on his face that she had never noticed before and more gray in his dark hair.

After the food had been passed around, Carly spoke up. "Nikki, Callan, I'm going home with Mom and Dad early tomorrow morning."

Aunt Marta quickly added, "But you and I will stay on

here another few days, Nikki, just like we planned originally."

Nikki grinned at Carly. "And I bet you're going to leave
all those makeover quizzes for me to finish, aren't you?"

Carly's smile turned a little sad, and she pushed the food
around on her plate with her fork before she spoke. "I think
maybe I need to worry more about what's going on under
the hood than trying so hard to paint the outside."

"Excuse me?" Dr. Phyllis said, her fork poised in midair.

Carly and Callan looked at each other and grinned, and
Carly said, "It's just something Callan told me that made me
think. I just have to start working on what's going on inside
me."

"And we'll all be working with you," Marlene Allen
said. "The whole family."

Carly shook her head. "I told you before, Mom, this is
my problem. I'm the one who's all messed up—"

"And we told you what we think of that theory," Dr.
Allen broke in. "These kinds of problems—eating disorders
and other problems like this—don't usually just pop up out
of nowhere. They grow out of the way family members
interact and relate to one another." He leaned across the
table, speaking as though they were alone in the kitchen.
"Remember what you said earlier this afternoon, Carly?
About feeling you could never measure up? But you
couldn't *tell* us so?"

Carly nodded, her brown eyes intent on his.

"I've been thinking about that all afternoon," Dr. Allen
continued. "It's hard to admit this, honey, but my own drive
to succeed got out of hand. I wanted each of you kids to
have high goals and achieve them, but somehow, even
while I thought I was communicating my love, what you
heard was that you had to be perfect or you couldn't earn
my love, or your mom's."

Dr. Allen lay down his fork and swallowed hard before speaking again. "And maybe, just maybe, you saw my pride. The pride that said, 'Don't you dare mess up and reflect badly on *me.*' Your mother's right, honey. We—the whole family—have a lot of talking to do, a lot of things to work through."

He looked around then and grinned self-consciously. "And I guess maybe I should quit acting like we're the only ones here." He turned to Marta. "This all hasn't put you too far behind on the book, has it?"

Marta laughed. "I'll catch up. I always did like a challenge. And Phyllis is a gold mine of information. She knows just about every folk musician east of the Mississippi. I think she's gotten me appointments with half of them in the next few days. I plan to wrap up the research just in time to get Nikki back to Michigan to start her senior year."

Epilogue

AUGUST 31

Dear Nikki,

I'm surviving!

You know how scared I was about facing people back at home, but everybody's being really nice. It's still hard for me to admit I have an "eating disorder." Every time I hear myself say that, I look around the room and wonder who on earth I'm talking about. It couldn't be me! But I guess it really is.

The doctors at this clinic have done all kinds of tests and asked me about a zillion questions. They finally told me today that I have bulimarexia, which means I switch back and forth from anorexia to bulimia.

We start family counseling tomorrow. I can't imagine how we're going to talk more, because that's all we've done for the last four days—talk, talk, talk!

The hardest part is, the "powers that be" have decided I have to be in a residence program at this center for people with eating disorders for the next couple months, so I'm just going to start my junior year there. If everything goes all right, the counselor and doctors say I may be able to go back to my old school after Christmas. I did enough crying about that already, so I won't get into it here. Besides, I'm supposed to be packing to leave. The center's only like two hours from my house, so my family can come to visit a lot. Everybody says this is what I need to do, so I'll give it my best shot.

I'm sorry I messed up our trip, Nikki. I already told your Aunt Marta and Dr. Phyllis how much I appreciated all they did, but could you just tell them again for me? They were both super, the way they arranged everything with my parents and all.

Callan said he'd write me while I'm at the center. I hate to admit it, Nik, but you were right. He really did turn out to be a decent guy. Sometimes when I feel like running away from this whole mess, I think about him and all he's had to face. And it helps.

Did Annie get permission to stay with Dr. Phyllis permanently yet? Did her dad get into the treatment program for his drinking? I think it's pretty amazing that Dr. Phyllis would offer to provide a home for her—let me know how it turns out, okay?

I'm writing Tory and Marissa after I finish this letter. I got them this crazy book I found called *How to Spoil Your New Cat Rotten*. It has a cat toy attached, and I'm sending them that.

Keep praying for me, would you, Nikki? Sometimes I'm awfully scared, and I know it'll be lonely at the center. But I want to face this thing now and get through it, instead of having it dog me for years.

I'll be in touch, you know that. I can't get E-mail at the center—not at first, anyway—so I'll send you my regular address as soon as I know it. Have to go finish packing.

Love,
Carly

If you or someone you know is struggling with an eating disorder, ask for books on the subject at your local Christian bookstore or call Focus on the Family at 1 (800) A–FAMILY to request resources.

The NIKKI SHERIDAN SERIES
by Shirley Brinkerhoff

9803

FOCUS ON THE FAMILY®

$\mathcal{L}$IKE THIS BOOK?